"On Your Feet!"

Tate spat on his hands and briskly rubbed them together. "I'm gonna stunt your growth and stomp all over you."

Starbuck flipped his cigarette and got to his feet. Tate uncorked a haymaker, and laid one upside his jaw.

The brassy taste of blood filled Starbuck's mouth, and he crashed over the chair. Tate launched a kick and he skittered away, rolling to his knees. On his feet again, Starbuck circled, feinted with his shoulder, and struck two splintering punches to the chin. Tate staggered, and Starbuck landed a hard clubbing right squarely between the eyes. The impact rocketed Tate across the room, then his eyes glazed and he slid to the floor, unmoving. Blood seeped down over his jaw. . . .

Matt Braun

HANGMAN'S CREEK

PUBLISHED BY POCKET BOOKS NEW YORK

Another *Original* publication of POCKET BOOKS

POCKET BOOKS, a Simon & Schuster division of
GULF & WESTERN CORPORATION
1230 Avenue of the Americas, New York, N.Y. 10020

ISBN 0-671-82031-1

First Pocket Books printing July, 1979

8   7   6   5   4   3   2   1

To
THE GANG
ALL OF THEM ACES HIGH
DORIS & DICK
BETTY & OTTO
DIANA & ED

Author's Note

Throughout the period 1875-1895 outlaw gangs roamed the western frontier, preying relentlessly on ranchers, stagecoach lines, railroads and banks. While the Wild Bunch and the Daltons gained the most notoriety, there were other renegade bands led by men of cunning and equal deadliness. The law was often stymied by vast distances and poor communications; no sooner was one gang routed than another appeared to take its place. Cattlemen's Associations, railroads and mine operators quickly discovered the futility of relying on local law enforcement officers. Instead they commenced hiring men who were cold-blooded and fast with a gun, and set them to hunting the outlaws. These men were the first of a breed—range detectives —and they were hindered neither by state boundaries nor the law itself. Their orders were to run the outlaws to earth, wherever the trail might lead, and see justice done. More often than not justice came at the end of a gun, for western desperadoes seldom surrendered when cornered.

Luke Starbuck was one such detective, and HANG-MAN'S CREEK is the story of his first manhunt. It is based on a true story.

CHAPTER ONE

Starbuck sat his roan gelding on a grassy knoll.

The sun was a fiery ball lodged in the sky and over the plains a shimmering haze hung like threads of spun glass. At noonday the heat was sweltering, and Starbuck's throat felt parched. He licked his lips, tasting salt, and took a swipe at his mustache. With one leg hooked around the saddlehorn, he watched the dusty melee of men and bawling calves on the prairie below. Spring roundup was under way, and several hundred cows had been gathered on a holding ground near the river. There the calves were roped, quickly separated from a herd of protesting mothers, and dragged to the branding fire. Working in teams, the cowhands swarmed over each calf after it was thrown. One man notched its ear with a knife, while another stepped forward with a white-hot iron, and moments later the calf scrambled away with LX seared on its flank. Hazed back to the herd by outriders, the calf was reunited with its mother, and ropes snaked out again under the broiling Texas sun.

The work was monotonous, a seemingly endless procession of calves from sunrise to sunset. Yet the cowhands never slackened their pace, and despite the heat, the branding went forward with smooth precision. For Luke Starbuck, it was merely one of several operations he would inspect in the course of a day. From early spring to late fall, the LX spread was a beehive of activity, and he was in the saddle almost constantly. As foreman of the largest ranch in the Panhandle, he was responsible for the crew, which numbered nearly a hundred men, and close to 50,000 cattle. Scattered around the ranch were a dozen branding camps, all working feverishly to tally and mark a fresh crop of spring calves. At the same time, separate crews were gathering grass-fattened steers and older cows for the trail drive to Dodge City. Before cold weather, at least ten herds, totaling more than 20,000 head, would be driven to railhead and sold. To the LX, it meant upward of $500,000 in the bank, and to Starbuck, it meant one long, unremitting headache that vanished only with the close of trailing season. He wouldn't have traded it for a rajah's palace and a harem of honey-tongued whores.

Since dawn, Starbuck had checked four branding camps and one of the trail herds. Altogether, he'd ridden better than fifty miles, twice swapping horses with remudas along the way, and he talked at length with each of the crew bosses. By sundown, when he reported to Ben Langham, the LX owner, he would have hit another four or five camps and have a pretty clear picture of the progress to date. All in all, he was satisfied with the way things were shaping up, and by rough estimate, he calculated it to be a very profitable season. Yet his report would be spotted with a touch of bad news, and the prospect dampened his mood. During the night, one of the branding camps had lost eight cow ponies out of its remuda, simply vanished without a trace. He'd given both the crew boss and the nighthawk a stiff reaming, and he would likly get a dose of the same himself later tonight—Ben Langham would be furious.

Still, he wasn't a man to dwell on problems, and it was a long way to sundown. He unhooked his leg from the saddlehorn and swung his boot into the stirrup. As he gathered the reins, about to ride down to the branding camp, a cowhand galloped over the knoll, spotting him at the last instant, and slid to a dust-smothered halt. Starbuck's roan shied away, dancing sideways across the slope, and he hauled back hard on the reins.

"What the hell's the rush?" he shouted through a curtain of dust. "Your pants on fire?"

"Damn near!" The rider was winded, and his horse lathered with sweat. He took a moment to catch his breath, then jerked a thumb over his shoulder. "The old man wants you—pronto!"

"What for?"

"Beats me, boss. He just come stormin' out of the house and I happened to be standin' in the way. Told me to light out damn quick, and not waste no time findin' you."

"How long ago?"

"Couple of hours. I missed you not more'n ten minutes over at the Blue Creek camp."

"Yeah, and goddamned near killed a horse in the bargain."

"Well hell's bells, boss, the old man said—"

"All right, you've found me. Now, get that horse cooled down, and do it right or you'll be walkin' home!"

Starbuck wheeled the roan away and rode east along the river. Slow to anger, he was nonetheless a stickler on certain things, and he wouldn't tolerate anyone who needlessly abused a horse. He made a mental note to have the cowhand draw his pay and clear out by morning. Then he put it from his mind, easing the roan into a steady lope, and turned his thoughts to Ben Langham.

Unless he read the sign wrong, the old man was on the war path. Whatever it was apparently couldn't wait until nightfall, and if it was that urgent, then it figured to be trouble of one sort or another. Good news could always wait; bad news travels fast. Over the years, by simple observation, he'd learned to anticipate the old man, most especially when there was trouble brewing. It was one of the reasons they got along so well, for Langham had a short fuse and a temper to match. Starbuck acted as a buffer, taking the brunt of his anger and then calmly setting right whatever had his nose out of joint. It saved everyone a world of grief, and had earned the old man's esteem in a manner he himself considered highly uncommon. He took delight in the fact that Starbuck could get people to swallow his orders with hardly a murmur of protest. He thought it a damn fine trick, and one of life's better jokes.

For his part, Starbuck thought it remarkable that Langham had never lost either his determination or his sense of humor. Several years past, Starbuck had hired on as a trailhand with the LX. At the time, Langham's spread was located in Southern Texas, less than a day's ride from the Rio Grande. A drifter, wandering aimlessly since the war, Starbuck had intended to work the season and then move on. But Langham saw qualities in the young saddle tramp that he'd never seen in himself. By the end of the season, Starbuck had been promoted to head wrangler, and charged with a sense of responsibility he'd never before experienced. The following season, when the youngster was jumped to trail boss and took a herd to Wichita, Langham's judgment was confirmed. Thereafter, year by year, Starbuck had assumed ever greater responsibility, until he

was promoted to segundo, second only to the LX foreman.

Then, during the summer of 1874, an outbreak of
cholera struck the ranch. Before the disease ran its
course, Langham's wife and three children, along with
the foreman and a score of cowhands, had fallen vic-
tim. The tragedy was compounded when Mexican
bandidos, with jackal-like cunning, took advantage of
the epidemic and intensified their raids from south of
the border. Devastated by the loss of his family, and
besieged by rustlers, Ben Langham sold out to the
King Ranch, which already controlled much of the Rio
Grande Valley. Yet, while he was determined to out-
distance memories of the past, his spirits were by no
means broken. Looking for a fresh start and a new
land, he turned his gaze north, to the Texas Panhandle.

There, on the banks of the Canadian River, he established a new ranch. Luke Starbuck, who had stuck
by him through it all, became foreman of the LX.
Within a year's time, a cattle herd had been trailed into the Panhandle, a main house and outbuildings were
raised, and Starbuck attracted top hands by paying top
wages. Though barely thirty when he assumed the job,
Starbuck had quickly earned the respect of every man
on the LX payroll. His knowledge of the cow business
was sufficient in most cases, and those hands foolish
enough to test a young foreman were soon persuaded
by his fists. After a couple of bunkhouse brawls, everybody decided he was chain lightning in a slug fest, and
an air of harmony settled over the ranch. Once again,
Ben Langham's faith in Starbuck's ability to handle
men and events had been confirmed.

To the south of the LX, Colonel Charles Goodnight
had already established a ranch along the eastern rim
of Palo Duro Canyon. With Langham's operation
thriving, and Goodnight running close to 100,000

head, other cattlemen were shortly attracted to the
Panhandle. When the Plains Tribes were herded onto
reservations in Indian Territory, thus removing the last
obstacle, there was a sudden influx of ranchers. Within
the last year, four cattlemen had settled around the
LX boundaries, and Langham had been instrumental
in forming the Panhandle Cattlemen's Association.
Charlie Goodnight, who ruled his own spread like a
medieval liege lord, had declined to join. Far from being offended, Langham thought it best for everyone
concerned. He'd had enough of cattle barons, and their
overbearing ways, along the Rio Grande. On the Canadian, with good neighbors and a spirit of coopera-
tion, he was convinced all would prosper equally.

In that, Luke Starbuck concurred heartily. After the
chaparral and mesquite thickets of southern Texas, the
boundless plains of the Panhandle seemed a cattleman's Eden. There was sweet grass and clear water,
vast prairies laced by streams feeding into the Canadian—everything western stockgrowers envisioned in
their most fanciful daydreams. It was what all men
searched for and few found—a land of milk and honey
and sweet green grass.

Today, riding toward the LX headquarters, Starbuck was reminded that much had been accomplished
in a brief span of time. Everywhere he looked there
were cattle, standing hock-deep in lush graze, with a
bountiful supply of water flowing endlessly eastward
along the Canadian. It warmed him with pride, know-
ing that he and Ben Langham, working together, had
created something substantial and enduring out of a
raw wilderness. Truly, for the first time in his life, he
felt a part of something, a nomad without family or
ties who had at last taken root. He felt at home, and
he felt a great debt to the man who had befriended a
stray, turned a brash fiddle-footed saddle tramp into

somebody—somebody who, in turn, had found himself.

All of which warmed his innards and gave him considerable pleasure. Yet fell short, now that he was approaching the ranch house, of quieting a curious sense of unease. Ben Langham was quick-tempered but hard as nails, not a man to be spooked. His summons today was all out of character, too urgent and somehow alarmed. It seemed to Starbuck an ominous sign. . . .

CHAPTER TWO

Ben Langham rose from his chair as Starbuck entered the study. Grouped around the desk were the four ranchers who, along with Langham, comprised the Panhandle Cattlemen's Association. The men turned but remained seated as Langham crossed the room. He paused before Starbuck, frowning, his voice lowered.

"Where the hell you been?"

"Tendin' cows."

"Well, you took your own sweet time gettin' here."

"Pushed right along," Starbuck informed him. "If you wanted me sooner, you should've sent for me sooner."

"Try mindin' your manners and don't give me any lip. I want these boys to think I'm still runnin' this outfit."

It was a standing joke between them. Age had begun to thicken Langham's waistline, but he still moved and spoke with vigor, and he was still very much in command of the LX. A bear of a man, he was an imposing figure, with a great mane of white hair and weathered features burned the dark mahogany of old saddle leather. Beside him, the young foreman appeared dwarfed in the shadow of a giant. Yet Starbuck was built along deceptive lines. He was corded and lean, all rawboned muscle, with a square jaw and faded blue eyes and lively chestnut hair. At first, men were fooled by his appearance, but not for long. Once they looked deeper into his eyes and observed his lithe catlike manner, their attitude changed. Life made many men hard and tough, brutalized them, but there was a greater difference, apparent upon closer examination. Luke Starbuck was dangerous.

After a moment, Langham turned, clapping an arm over Starbuck's shoulders, and walked forward with a broad grin. "Luke, say howdy to the boys. No strangers here, so we won't stand on ceremony. Grab yourself a chair and take a load off your feet."

Starbuck sat down warily, the way a hawk perches on a branch. The men nodded, greeting him by name, but he was aware of an undercurrent, something unspoken in their manner. Will Rutledge and Vernon Pryor were seated on his right, Oscar Gilchrist and Earl Musgrave on the opposite side; his chair was centered on the desk and he felt crowded, acutely uncomfortable, almost as though he were on display. Yet he never indulged in small talk or encouraged it in others, and no one thought it unusual now that he held his silence. While Langham circled the desk, he took out the makings and started building himself a smoke. As he finished rolling and licked the paper, there was a moment of leaden stillness. Langham settled back in his chair, the smile slowly fading, and stared across the desk. Finally, with a heavy grunt, he hitched forward.

"Luke, we've got a problem, helluva problem." Langham waved his hand at the ranchers. "Every one of these boys was hit by horse thieves within the past week. Lost more'n forty head between 'em."

Starbuck struck a match on his thumbnail, lit the cigarette. "Guess that makes it unanimous." He snuffed the match, tossed it in an ashtray. "We lost eight head over at the Blue Creek camp last night."

"Last night! They hit us last night? Well, why in the samhill didn't you tell me?"

"Never gave me a chance. Besides, I only found out about it myself this morning."

"That settles it!" Langham's fist slammed into the desk. "By God, boys, we'll nail those bastards and hang 'em out to dry. Damned if we won't."

"Sooner the better!" Will Rutledge added hotly. "Sonsabitches gotta be stopped or they're gonna ruin us certain."

The others murmured agreement, nodding among themselves, then turned their attention to Langham. He looked around, studying their faces a moment, before his gaze fell on Starbuck. His expression was grave, and very earnest.

"Luke, me and the boys have been in a powwow all mornin', and we've decided it's time we took things in our own hands. That's why I sent for you."

Starbuck took a long drag, watching him, and slowly exhaled smoke. "I've got an idea I won't like it, but go ahead . . . I'm listening."

"Well, you see, it's like this, we talked it out and we've agreed—"

"I haven't agreed to nothin'!" Earl Musgrave broke in. "Leastways, not yet."

"All right, Earl, duly noted. But we took a vote and it still stands."

"Vote?" Starbuck frowned. "What kind of vote?"

"Now, Luke, we've all been losin' horses, I don't have to tell you that. But it's gotten damn serious, 'specially when you consider all the time and money invested in a good cow pony. Way we calculate it, we've lost upward of three hundred head in the last six months, and that ain't chickenfeed. We're talkin' about better'n $50,000!"

"Yeah, I know, but let's get to the part about the vote."

"I'm comin' to that," Langham assured him. "I just want you to understand the problem. We're way the hell out here in the middle of nowhere—with no law closer'n a four-day ride—and somebody's stealin' our horses regular as clockwork. We've got to put a stop to it!"

"You're greasin' the chute, Ben. What's the point?"

Langham sighed, looked him straight in the eye. "We need a range detective, Luke, need one bad. I sort of volunteered you for the job."

Starbuck was genuinely surprised. "That's real thoughtful of you, but why me? Hell, I'm no lawman."

"See there!" Musgrave crowed. "Same thing I've been tryin' to tell you the whole damn day."

"Awww, for Chrissakes!" Langham groaned. "He's meaner'n tiger spit, and everybody knows it. There ain't a man within a hundred miles that'd tangle with him. Go on, answer me that if you're so damn smart . . . *is there?*"

"Maybe not," Musgrave conceded. "But that don't mean he's got a taste for raw meat. What we need is a bounty hunter . . . a professional."

"You seem to have forgot he served with Rip Ford durin' the war. I reckon he's killed his share and then some. Ain't that right, Luke?"

"Yeah, a few," Starbuck agreed. "But I can't say I exactly developed a taste for it."

"Told you so!" Musgrave bobbed his head with a smug grin. "Fistfights are one thing. . . . Huntin' men down and hangin' them—that's a different ball of wax altogether."

"Goddamnit, Earl, why don't you leave well enough alone?"

Langham's brushy eyebrows drew together in a scowl. He leaned across the desk and stabbed at Musgrave with his finger. "We done decided, and that's that! So just button your lip and let's get on with it. Savvy?"

For a moment, the two men glared at each other, and an uneasy silence fell over the room. Then Vernon Pryor cleared his throat, broke the stalemate. He was a man of glacial calm, tall and bony with distinguished features. He seldom spoke, and as a result, the other men attached a certain weight to his opinion.

"I agree with Ben," Pryor told them. "We need a man of our own—not some outsider—and to my way of thinking, Luke fits the ticket."

"Hold off!" Starbuck interjected. "Before we go too far, I'd still like an answer to my question. Why me?"

"Several reasons," Langham replied. "You've got the backbone for the job, and we know you'll see it through. But I reckon Vern hit the one that counts the most. You see, we trust you, Luke. It's as simple as that."

"What he's trying to say," Pryor added, "is that we don't want the law involved. We intend to deal with these thieves in our own way."

"Damn right!" Oscar Gilchrist growled. "Give 'em a stiff rope and a short drop!"

"In other words," Starbuck noted, "you're talkin' about Judge Lynch. No trial, no jury . . . no nothin'?"

"String 'em up," Rutledge flared, "and have done with it! We want it ended neat and tidy—ended permanent—and the law would only complicate things."

"It ain't pretty," Langham observed, "but he's right, Luke. The nearest court's in Fort Worth, and a jury of shopkeepers and ribbon clerks ain't about to look at horse thieves the way we do. You know it yourself; city folks just don't understand that when you steal a man's horse and put him afoot out here, you've the same as murdered him."

"Yeah, sometimes," Starbuck admitted. "But we're talkin' about herd stock, not a man's personal horse."

"Judas Priest!" Langham thundered. "You've got to draw the line! Besides which, we ain't got time to sit around a courtroom and wind up with a jury givin' 'em a couple of years in the pen. We need an object lesson, and we need it goddamn quick! Otherwise, we'll look like easy pickin's to every sonovabitch with a long rope and a runnin' iron."

"Luke knows that," Pryor said in a reasonable tone. "Unless we deal harshly with horse thieves, then we're simply invitin' trouble from cattle rustlers, and we can't afford to let it get out of hand. Don't you agree, Luke?"

"No argument there, none at all."

Langham gave him a dour look. "Then suppose you tell us what the hell's botherin' you. I figgured you'd be keen for the job, or I wouldn't've called you in here."

"Why, it's simple enough," Starbuck remarked. "You aim to hang whoever I point my finger at. That's a pretty heavy load, and to tell you the truth, I don't much like the idea of playin' God."

There was a moment of deliberation, then Langham shook his head. "Maybe I know you better'n you know yourself. Unless you was plumb goddamn certain, you'd wait till hell froze over before you pointed your finger. Now, ain't that a plain fact?"

Starbuck shrugged. "Yeah, I reckon you've got a point there."

"Then we're of a mind," Langham said with assurance. "You take your time and don't worry about yell-in' sic 'em until you're dead-sure satisfied. Sound fair?"

Starbuck took a long drag on his cigarette, thoughtful. At last, exhaling smoke, he leaned forward and stubbed out the butt in an ashtray.

"Who would you get to ramrod the ranch?"

"Don't trouble yourself about it. Jack Noonan's made you a good segundo, and I'll work close with him while you're gone."

"You're sayin' I'll come back as foreman . . . when it's finished?"

"Hell, it's yours as long as you want it." Langham paused, suddenly chuckled. " 'Course, you never know. Maybe you'll get to like bein' a manhunter."

"Maybe," Starbuck allowed. "Reckon we'll have to wait and see."

"You'll take the job, then?"

"Yeah, I'll give it a try." Starbuck cocked one eyebrow, squinted at him hard. "So long as we're agreed it's not permanent."

"You've got my word on it, straight down the line."

"All right, when do I start?"

"Now by God! We're already a day late and a dollar short."

Langham unfurled an oilskin map and spread it across his desk. "Have a looksee. I'll explain what we've got in mind and you take it from there."

Starbuck rose and stepped forward, his gaze fixed on the map. The ranchers gathered around and Langham began talking. His finger jabbed at an X marked on the oilskin, then another and still another, tracing a line along the Red River. Starbuck smiled, nodding, not at all surprised by the old man's craft. It was a good plan, simple but tricky, and even a little appealing.

A plan tailored perfectly for a former saddle tramp.

CHAPTER THREE

After supper that evening, Starbuck stripped to the waist and stepped out to the washbasins in front of the bunkhouse. He lathered his face, peering into a faded mirror tacked to the wall, and shaved with a freshly stropped razor. Then he scrubbed his upper body with the soapy water, washing away an accumulation of sweat and grime, and toweled dry. Wetting his hair, he gave it a few licks with a comb and studied himself in the mirror. He had little vanity, but the inspection convinced him he'd done a passable job, considering his hard-planed features. He knuckled back his mustache, gathered his gear, and returned to the bunkhouse.

Several minutes later he emerged dressed in his good shirt and the hand-tooled boots generally reserved for dances and church socials. Some of the men were loafing out front, and he took a bit of good-natured ribbing as he walked toward the corral. Since he seldom left the ranch on weeknights, their comments were perhaps more ribald than usual. But Starbuck wasn't offended, nor did he acknowledge their remarks. He'd learned long ago that most men, cowhands in particular, only joked with someone they genuinely liked. For his part, he knew it kept them uncertain and slightly off balance if he simply ignored the jibes. That was his joke, and certain men thought him humorless, aloof. Yet, in his quiet way, he was something of a jester. He preferred to outwit them rather than outtalk them.

By the time he was saddled, the sun went down over the river in a great splash of orange and gold. He mounted and rode north into the gathering dusk. The main house was already ablaze with lamplight, and it made him laugh to think of the old man lecturing Jack Noonan. Before morning, the entire crew would know they had a new foreman, and the thought prompted an even deeper chuckle. Cowhands were inveterate grumblers, thrived on it. The sudden switchover would set them rumbling like a flock of scalded owls.

One thought triggered another, and the smile slowly dissolved. Starbuck realized he wasn't all that easy about the arrangement himself. It was a challenge— the biggest of his life!—and that part intrigued him. But it was a whole new world, far afield from bossing a cattle outfit. Though he hadn't admitted it to Langham or the others, he was bluntly honest with himself. He still had a few qualms about his prospects as a range detective. Or, to put the word on it that better fitted ... a manhunter.

Not that the idea of a hanging bothered him. On that score, Langham had him pretty well pegged. He'd ridden with Colonel Rip Ford's volunteer cavalry all through the war. Scarcely seventeen when he joined up, he'd learned quick enough that killing was merely a peculiar sort of habit, easily cultivated. In the heat of battle, with Yankee troopers intent on killing him, he had experienced no difficulty whatever. At first, it was a matter of being scared and simply fighting for his life. Later, after he'd taught himself to master fear, it became a natural, and very elemental, form of anger. It just made him damned mad that anyone would try to douse his lights. Nor was his anger merely the anger of war, limited to Bluebellies. Once, in a dispute over cards, he'd killed a tinhorn in a Brownsville saloon. If anything, it was more satisfying than the men he had slain on the battlefield, for it was a very personal thing with the gambler, face to face across a poker table. By the summer of 1865, when Union troops officially occupied the Rio Grande, he was a seasoned veteran of the killing ground. Blooded himself, having been wounded in three separate engagements, he had grown somewhat fatalistic regarding the possibility of his own death. As for spilling blood, he'd long since lost the queasy sensation. Pulling the trigger on another man wasn't easy, but then neither was it difficult. It was an acquired habit, like tobacco or hard liquor.

Yet there was a vast difference between killing men and hunting them down. One required only the twitch of a finger; the other demanded skill and persistence and a certain amount of guile. Starbuck wasn't at all sure he had the flair for such work. Deception simply wasn't his strong suit, and he had no knack for turning the other cheek. If someone curried him the wrong way, he promptly dusted their skull and pondered the wisdom of it later. With outlaws, of course, that wouldn't work. He'd have to take it slow and easy, pick up their trail with no one the wiser. Then, once he found them, it would be necessary to worm his way into their confidence. All that would require some mighty convincing lies, and a tight grip on himself at all times. Even the simplest lapse, one unguarded moment, would expose his hand . . . and probably get him killed.

It was a dicey proposition. One with long odds and damned little room for error. A regular bear trap of a

job, especially for a man unfamiliar with the tricks
and dodges of those who rode the owl hoot. Still,
Ben Langham thought he could pull it off, and the old
man had never been wrong before. As a matter of fact,
there in the meeting today, he'd actually touched a
nerve. Perhaps more than he realized at the time.

Starbuck sort of liked the idea of turning manhunter.
He hadn't yet put his thumb on the exact reason, and
whether or not the feeling would last was anyone's
guess. But tonight he had a hunch, a good hunch. He
meant to follow it.

An hour later Starbuck dismounted in the yard of
the Pryor ranch. On the porch, seated in rockers, were
Vernon Pryor and his wife. Starbuck figured the younger
children were already in bed, but he hadn't thought
Janet would retire so early. He cursed under his
breath, wondering if he'd ridden all that way for nothing. As he looped the reins around the hitch rack,
Pryor rose and walked to the edge of the porch.

"Good evening, Luke."

"Evenin'." Starbuck moved to the steps, touching
the brim of his hat as he glanced into the shadows.
"Evenin', Mrs. Pryor. How are you tonight?"

"Tolerable, thank you. Just tolerable."

Agnes Pryor was a lumpy woman, with big slack
breasts and widespread hips. Her husband looked almost skeletal by comparison, and Starbuck had always thought it a curious match: a bit like a greyhound
and a brood sow. Yet it was revealing in other ways,
especially where the Pryors' oldest daughter was concerned. He knew that Janet, given a few years, would
turn out very much like her mother. He kept the image
fresh in mind whenever he came calling.

Pryor knocked the dottle from his pipe, smiled.
"Guess you're here to see Janet?"

Starbuck nodded. "Thought I'd say goodbye, unless it's too late. She still up?"

"Oh, don't worry about that. She's expecting you—has been since sundown."

"She knows I'm leavin', then?"

"I told her when I got home."

Pryor's smile widened. Watching him, Starbuck thought he appeared awfully pleased with himself. There had never been any discussion about Janet—or his intentions—but neither had he been made to feel welcome here. He got the sudden impression that Pryor wouldn't be unhappy to see him leave.

"Does she know I'm liable to be gone a while?"

"Yes. I told her that, too. She asked, and I saw no reason to shade the truth."

"No reason at all." Starbuck paused, considering. "How'd she take the news . . . about the job?"

"Why don't you ask me yourself?"

Janet Pryor emerged from the door, framed in a spill of light. She was a robust girl, with a wide mouth and apple cheeks and deepset dimples. Her hair was parted in the middle and drawn back in a bun, with a cluster of golden curls fluffed high on her forehead. Normally, she was engaging and eager to please, but tonight her eyes were flecked with greenfire. As she crossed the porch, Starbuck noted she was sulled up, the gingham gown stretched taut across her breasts.

"Evenin', Jan." Starbuck doffed his hat. "Thought I'd surprise you, but your dad tells me—"

"Daddy, Mama"—Janet stepped off the porch and walked past him—"would you excuse us? We have some talking to do."

Pryor gave him a cadaverous grin, and Starbuck hurried after the girl. When he caught up, she ignored him, looking straight ahead. At a quick pace, her

stride determined, she crossed the yard. Without another word, they disappeared into the darkness.

A brisk walk brought them to a creek south of the
house. Huge live oaks sheltered the grassy bank, and
in months past, it had been their trysting place. But
tonight there was no warmth in Janet's manner. She
halted, arms folded at the waist, and stared into the
water for several moments. At last, she turned on him,
her face masked with anger.

"You've certainly got your nerve, Luke Starbuck!"

"Yeah, I thought you might be a little upset."

"A little upset!" she cried. "You think that's all it
amounts to?"

"C'mon, it's only a job. No need to get yourself
worried before I've even started."

"Worried? I'm not worried, Luke—I'm mad!"

"Oh." Starbuck looked puzzled. "I don't get it . . .
mad about what?"

"Don't play the fool with me! We had an understanding, and now I find out you practically jumped
at this job."

"Well, it's honest work and the pay's good. Nothing
wrong with that."

"Stop it!" she demanded in an insistent voice. "Do
you really think I intend to marry a . . . bounty hunter
. . . do you?"

Starbuck thought it unlikely. Which was one of the
reasons he'd accepted the job. Within the last few
months, he had begun to feel trapped. She was making
great plans for the future—their future—and he wasn't
at all sure the arrangement suited him. Yet a man
should be dead certain before entering into anything
that permanent. He needed time to think things out,
and the new job seemed somehow providential. Away

from her, off on his own again, perhaps he'd find he couldn't do without her. On the other hand . . .

"Guess your mind's pretty well set, hmm?"

"No, it's not! I'm confused and hurt and I don't understand, Luke. I just don't understand why you're doing it!"

"Whatever my reasons, you're definite about not marrying a bounty hunter, aren't you?"

"Yes! I most certainly am, very definite!"

"Thought so." He deliberated a moment, then shrugged his shoulders and smiled. "Well, in that case, maybe you'd consider foolin' around with a range detective."

"Oh . . . you . . . you sneaky bastard!"

Janet turned away in a huff. But she made no attempt to leave, and after a moment Starbuck stepped forward. He took her arms and slowly pulled her around. Though she offered little resistance, she refused to look at him directly. He cupped her chin in his hand, gently lifted her mouth to his, and kissed her. Then he nuzzled her ear, his voice warm and husky.

"One thing I promise you—I'll come back."

"How nice!" she sniffed. "Am I supposed to sit around and pine while you're gone?"

"It won't take long, couple of weeks at the outside." Starbuck smiled, very earnest now. "That's what I've been tryin' to tell you, the job's not permanent. I've got Langham's word on it."

"Honestly?" Her eyes brightened. "You'll still be foreman of the LX . . . he told you that . . . agreed to it?"

"Anytime I want it. And you know the old man, his word's good as gold."

She glanced aside. "That's not what my father said, Luke. He told me wild horses couldn't have stopped you."

"Hell, him and Langham are the ones that talked me into it."

"Really and truly—you swear it, Luke—it was their idea?"

"For a fact!" Starbuck assured her. "Your dad wants to see me long gone . . . or haven't you figured that out yet?"

"I know," she murmured. "He thinks we're . . . well . . . that I like you too much."

"How about you?" Starbuck asked. "What do you think?"

Janet held his gaze for a long while. She scrutinized him openly, searching for any trace of guile, but his look was level, steadfast. Finally, she put her arms around his neck and smiled.

"I think I'm going to miss you every minute you're away."

Starbuck drew her into a close embrace. Her mouth met his greedily, and her tongue parted his lips, at once inviting and teasing. He lifted her in his arms, slowly lowered her to the grassy bank, and eased down beside her. A tangle of arms and legs, breathing hard, they came together in a frenzied clash. His hand touched bare flesh, crept higher beneath her dress, and she moaned. Along the creek the katydids fell silent. Then he levered himself on top of her and she cried out and the night sounds ceased altogether. Starlight filtered dimly through the trees, and their shapes were blurred, joined as one . . .

A long time.

CHAPTER FOUR

Starbuck rode into Tahlequah early in June.

The sky was like dull pewter, threatening rain, and the road leading into town was rutted iron. Directly ahead, across the town square, was the capitol building of the Cherokee Nation. It was a large, two-story brick structure, with a sweeping portico in front, and it dominated a thriving business district. There was an air of bustling efficiency about the place, and to Starbuck's amazement, a group of men gathered on the capitol steps were dressed in swallowtail coats and top hats. In contrast, his own clothes were caked with sweat and grime, and bearded stubble covered his jaw. He'd been on the trail nearly three weeks, and he hadn't had a bath since the last time it rained.

The path that led him to Tahlequah had been long and frustrating, an odyssey of sorts. Upon departing the LX in late May, he had ridden directly to Fort Sumner, in New Mexico Territory. With Billy the Kid on the rampage—leading a gang of veteran rustlers—it seemed the most likely spot to look for stolen horses. But a few days' inquiry quickly convinced him it was a washout. The Kid was a cold-blooded killer, with a price on his head, and conducted will-o'-the-wisp raids whenever it struck his fancy. Still, for all his brash daring, the Kid had never been known as a horse thief. His specialty was cattle . . . and murder—not cow ponies.

Turning eastward, Starbuck had then followed a meandering course along the Red River. At Doan's Store and Red River Station, the main crossings for cattle drives to Kansas, he had paused briefly. Posing as a saddle tramp, he was able to make discreet inquiries, and soon satisfied himself that there was little commerce in stolen horses. Still holding to Ben Langham's plan, he'd next turned northeast into Indian Territory. Yet he uncovered nothing in either the Chickasaw Nation or the Choctaw Nation, and within the week, he'd headed due north toward Tahlequah. By then, his hopes were rapidly diminishing, and as he crossed the Cherokee Nation, his mood darkened. Altogether, he'd ridden better than a thousand miles, without unearthing so much as a single lead. It suddenly seemed futile, a damnedable waste of time. He was searching in the wrong direction.

Not that he wasn't enjoying himself. The old wanderlust of days past had once again taken hold, and he found it an exhilarating sensation. Since leaving the LX, he'd given only scant thought to Janet Pryor, and in all honesty, he simply hadn't missed her. Nor had he experienced any great yearning for the ranch itself. Curiously, it was as though an enormous burden had been lifted from his shoulders. Until he was away from it, he'd had no idea of how heavily the responsibility weighed. Over the years he had gradually convinced himself it was the kind of life he wanted; with Ben Langham as an image, and ever-greater responsibility the lodestar, he had been beguiled into accepting a role totally foreign to his character. With only a few weeks freedom, out on his own again, he'd come to a sharp awakening. By nature, he was a loner, perfectly willing to answer for his own actions but uncomfortable when saddled with the responsibility of others. For the first time in almost twelve years, he felt unfettered and at ease deep within himself. He now had grave doubts about the life he'd led all that time. High on the list was the LX . . . and Janet Pryor.

Yet he wasn't a man to shirk obligation. He'd accepted a job and he meant to see it through. Time enough to settle his personal affairs—one way or another—once he'd run the horse thieves to earth. All of which kindled a wry smile. Considering his luck to date, that looked to be a long and lonely chore.

Crossing the town square, Starbuck was reminded that he was very much the outsider here. A strange white man drew stares of suspicion and hostility anywhere in Indian Territory. The Five Civilized Tribes had suffered grievously at the hands of whites, perhaps none more so than the Cherokees. Except through intermarriage, white men were not allowed to own property within the Nations. Nor were they welcome as visitors, unless the courts had branded them outlaws. By some twisted logic, a white businessman, however scrupulous, was thought to be less trustworthy than a white desperado. All too often the Cherokees connived with outlaws, offering them asylum from federal marshals, and that made Starbuck's task all the more difficult. The Cherokees felt a bond of affinity with anyone who flouted the white man's law, and they resented nosy intruders. He had to be careful about the questions he asked. Very careful indeed.

On a sidestreet, Starbuck dismounted in front of a livestock dealer. Several mules were bunched in a corral at one end of the building, but there were no horses in sight. As Starbuck walked forward, a man appeared in the doorway. He had a cured look, as

though he'd been dipped in a tanning vat and left too
long. His features were angular, with a hawk-like nose
and high cheekbones, and his jaw was loaded solid with
chewing tobacco. He worked his quid, eyes expression-
less, offering no greeting.

"Howdy." Starbuck nodded. "Wonder if I could have
a word with the owner?"

"You're looking at him."

"Well, good, glad to hear it. Thought maybe you
could help me out."

"How so?"

"I'm a wrangler lookin' for work. Figured you
might know somebody that needs a top hand."

The dealer shifted his cud and spat. A puff of dust
exploded in the dirt. Then he jerked his head toward
the corral. "You see any horses out there?"

"Nope, can't say as I do."

"Guess that answers your questions."

"Yeah, maybe it does." Starbuck pulled at his ear
studied the mules a moment. " 'Course, it could be
you've just sold off all your horses."

The dealer uttered a noncommittal grunt.

"Any outfit that buys lots of horses, you'd be doing
them a favor. Like I told you, I'm a top hand, that's
no brag."

"And I already told you, times are slow."

"Come on, you mean to say nobody's hirin' in these
parts?"

There was a moment of deliberation, then the dealer
fixed him with a hard look. "You ask a lot of questions . . . for a white man."

Starbuck met his gaze, eyes impersonal, but seething
inside. Finally, with a tight grip on his temper, he
turned and walked to his horse. As he stepped into the
saddle, he glanced back at the dealer and smiled.

"Mister, you've been a real help, and I'm obliged. Won't forget your courtesy, that's for sure."

With a curt nod, Starbuck reined the gelding around and rode toward the square. He felt the dealer's eyes boring into his back, and congratulated himself on his restraint. A skulldusting would have done the man a world of good, perhaps taught him to watch his mouth. But it was better to leave peaceable, without drawing attention to himself. All the same, it was hard to swallow.

Entering the square, Starbuck proceeded west, past the capitol building. As he rode by, the group of men on the steps fell silent, watching him closely. From their dress, he assumed they were legislators, and it occurred to him that the Five Civilized Tribes were aptly named. The Cherokee Nation was, for all practical purposes, an independent republic. With slight variations, the tribe's form of government was patterned on that of the white man. A tribal chief was elected head of state, and the legislative body, called the tribal council, was comprised of two houses, similar in function to the U.S. Congress. It all appeared very democratic, and highly civilized. Yet there remained a hard core of hatred toward white men, and that seemed to him a real puzzler. Folks seldom aped their enemies . . . enlightened or otherwise.

Starbuck put it from mind and turned his thoughts to business. Now, more than ever, he was convinced the direction of his search must shift westward. By pushing it, he could reach Fort Supply in perhaps four days, and that would be his last stop in Indian Territory. Unless the army had evidence to the contrary, he seriously doubted the Comanches were conducting secret raids into the Panhandle. That being the case, he meant to turn north, toward Dodge City. If he drew a blank there, then he'd have little choice but to write Ben Langham and broaden the search into Colorado. Some inner hunch—strengthened by his miserable luck thus far—told him Colorado was where he should have started in the first place. But ahead lay Fort Supply and Dodge. If not by deduction, then by process of elimination he would gradually whittle down the possibilities. As he rode out of town, he wondered if real detectives went about their work in a similar manner. He thought not.

Several miles west of Tahlequah, the Light Horse Police overtook him. There were five of them, led by a hard-eyed sergeant, and they came on at a gallop, surrounding him before he realized their intent. One look convinced him it wasn't routine, but he couldn't believe they meant to arrest him. Nonetheless, he kept his hands in plain sight, firmly anchored to the reins.

"What's your name?" the sergeant demanded. "Your real name?"

"Starbuck. Lucas Starbuck. Only name I've got."

"Where you from?"

"Texas, mostly, or leastways I was. Been driftin' around, lookin' for work."

"How come a top-hand wrangler can't find work in Texas?"

Starbuck warned himself to proceed cautiously. It was no accident he'd been pursued, that much was now apparent. The Light Horse Police were rough customers, known for dispensing summary justice at trailside. Whatever the reason, he was in a touchy spot, and it was no time to go off half-cocked. He shrugged.

"Got a case of itchy feet, simple as that. Work awhile, drift awhile, that's my motto."

"Why you ask so many questions about horses?"

"Say, look here, I never meant to rub that fellow back in town the wrong way. But, hell's bells, he wasn't very polite, and that's a fact."

"Don't talk, just gimme straight answers."

"Judas Priest, horses are my line of work! He must've told you that."

The sergeant eyed him a moment, then rapped out a sharp command. "The truth—don't lie—how long ago you leave Fort Smith?"

"Fort Smith?" Starbuck glanced around, found himself ringed by cold stares. "Wait a minute, boys, you've got me mixed up with somebody else. Hell, I've never been to Fort Smith."

"You lie! All Judge Parker's men lie! Got no business here!"

"Well, I'll be damned! You think I work for Parker, don't you? You actually think I'm a marshal!"

Starbuck's expression was one of genuine surprise. Along with it was a look of mild relief, and the combination left the sergeant momentarily confounded. Then he scowled, muddy brown eyes alive with hate.

"No more talk! You keep ridin' and don't bother Cherokees no more."

He paused, lips skinned back in an arrogant grin. "Or maybe the Judge lose himself a marshal."

Starbuck bristled, unaccustomed to threats. But the odds were bad and the timing even worse. Better to let them think what they wanted and be on his way. Particularly since it wasn't his fight, anyway. He stared at the sergeant for a moment, then nodded and reined his gelding around. The Light Horse Police broke their ring, backing their mounts aside, and sat watching as he rode off along the rutted trail.

Some distance away, Starbuck suddenly chuckled to himself. It was ironic as hell! The Hanging Judge and his U.S. Marshals were considered pure poison in Indian Territory. All across the West, Judge Isaac Parker was celebrated for his love of hemp and his dispassionate attitude toward Indian lawbreakers.

Only last year, with a thousand or more spectators looking on, he had hung six men with one spring of the trap. And three of them Cherokees! Small wonder that his very name raised hackles in Tahlequah. But Starbuck found it grimly amusing that he'd been mistaken for one of Parker's manhunters. Apparently, there was more to this detective business than he'd suspected. Had to be, for it was clear now that he had fooled the livestock dealer too well.

Almost too well for his own good.

CHAPTER FIVE

Under the brassy dome of a plains sky, Starbuck reined to a halt. After removing his hat, he pulled a filthy bandanna and mopped his face. The Kansas prairie shimmered with heat waves, a vast grassland that seemed to extend onward into eternity. He shaded his eyes with the hat and regarded the angle of the sun. Three o'clock, perhaps a bit later, and Dodge City still fifty miles up the trail. Unless he found a stream, it meant a dry camp tonight, even though his canteen was nearly full. The prospect did little to improve his mood.

Stuffing the bandanna into his hip pocket, he crammed the hat on his head. Then he gathered the reins, feathering the gelding with his spurs, and rode north. Behind him lay a week's hard riding, and the deep conviction he'd wasted the past month on a wild-goose chase. So far as he could determine, horse-stealing was fast becoming a lost art in Indian Territory. Even the Comanches, once considered the supreme horse thieves of all the Plains tribes, were content with government handouts and the idleness of reservation life. It was a sorry state of affairs, and, for a tyro manhunter, downright discouraging.

Shortly before dawn that morning, he had left Fort Supply. A day there, spent in casual conversation with a grizzled master sergeant and several troopers, had merely confirmed what he already suspected. The Comanches and Kiowas, who traditionally raided into Texas, had become tame Indians, wholly dependent on the government for their subsistence. His hunch stronger than ever, he had turned north, skirting the Western Trail. It was the height of the cattle season, and the trail was choked with Texas longhorns; he avoided the dust and confusion, preferring to strike overland and make better time. By early afternoon, he had forded a dogleg in the Cimarron River, which placed him roughly ten miles above the Kansas border. While he was hot and weary, drenched in sweat from the blazing June sun, he felt a renewed surge of determination once across the Cimarron. Ahead lay Dodge City, one last stop before he ditched Langham's plan and headed for Colorado. It was a fresh start, almost as though he'd just begun the hunt.

Yet now, with the sun slipping westward, his exuberant mood slowly faded. Though he'd been up the Western Trail several times, the open prairie was a complete mystery. Boundless and parched, it swept on with an undulating sameness that left a man mesmerized. He was by no means lost, for the cardinal points of the compass were like a sixth sense, born of a lifetime spent in wilderness terrain. But a dry camp, with one canteen to be shared with his horse, promised an uncomfortable night. Worse, it meant no coffee tomorrow morning, and perhaps a long, thirsty ride to Dodge. He kneed the gelding into a trot and began scanning the distance for a treeline. Trees and creeks often went together, and with several hours of daylight left, anything was possible. Even morning coffee.

Late that afternoon he topped a rise and suddenly

pulled up short. Below was a grove of trees, bordered
by a stream, and off to one side stood a clapboard
house and a barn with a log corral. A wagon road
snaked westward, and to the north he saw a herd of
cattle grazing on a level stretch of prairie. It looked to
be a small operation, perhaps a couple of hundred
head, but somebody had picked a choice location.
With water in sight, and morning coffee assured, his
spirits took a sharp upturn. He tickled the gelding's
ribs and rode toward the house.

Several minutes later Starbuck crossed the stream
and spotted two men outside the corral. A horse was
tied to the log fence and an enclosed wagon was
parked nearby. While one man, obviously a farrier,
worked on the horse's hooves, the other man lounged
against the fence. As Starbuck rode closer, the men
glanced around, regarding him with a speculative look.
Then the blacksmith went back to fitting a shoe, and
the other man pushed off the fence, walking forward.
By his dress—worn boots and faded range clothes—
he appeared to be a cowman. His legs, bowed like
barrel staves, merely confirmed the impression. He
nodded, eyes squinted and watchful, as Starbuck
reined to a halt.

"Howdy."

"Afternoon."

Starbuck waited, allowing himself to be inspected.
Since range etiquette required an invitation, he made
no move to dismount. With a practiced eye, the man
quickly scrutinized clothes and horse and trappings.
At last, satisfied with what he saw, his manner
thawed.

" 'Pears you've had a long ride."

"Long and thirsty," Starbuck replied. "Not a helluva lot of water between here and the Cimarron."

"That's a fact," the man agreed. " 'Course, you're

a little off the track, leastways if I read your rig right. We don't see many Texans over in this direction."

Starbuck smiled. "Tell you the truth, I got fired off a trail drive. Nothin' serious, you understand, but me and the ramrod sort of parted company." He shrugged. "Figured I'd have a looksee at Kansas on my way into Dodge."

"Been up the trail a few times myself. Finally got a gutful and married a widder woman. Her and her spread." He pursed his mouth, cocked one eye. "Ain't much, but it beats thirty a month and beans."

"Looks mighty good to me. Your wife wouldn't have a sister, would she?"

"Hah! Had your fill of eatin' dust, have you?"

"Enough for one day, no doubt about it."

"Well, light and tie, make yourself to home."

"Much obliged." Starbuck stepped down out of the saddle. "If you've got no objection, I wouldn't mind pitchin' camp on your stream for the night."

"Help yourself." He stuck out his hand. "Name's Clute Jordan."

"Luke Starbuck."

Jordan was a wiry man, with gnarled features and a beard so thick that his face resembled a good-humored cockleburr. He grinned and pumped Star-buck's hand.

"Whyn't you unsaddle and hobble your horse on that grassy stretch by the creek? I got some of mine gettin' shod, and the smith only gets out this way ever' couple of months, so I'm sorta tied up. You're welcome to join us, though, if you're of a mind."

"Thanks, I'll do that."

A while later, after he'd watered the gelding and left him to graze, Starbuck walked back to the corral. Jordan greeted him and nodded at the farrier, who was toasting a horseshoe in a steel-plated portable forge.

"This here's Sam Urschel. Best damn smith in Kansas. Sam, meet Luke Starbuck."

Urschel was a large man, heavy through the shoulders, and given to few words. He grunted something unintelligible, then began hammering the cherry-red shoe on an anvil bolted to the rear of the wagon. Starbuck watched a moment, then turned his attention to the horse, a dun gelding standing hipshot at the fence. Out of habit, he checked confirmation and weight, judging the dun at a hair over fourteen hands. Small but with good bottom, built for catlike turns and short bursts of speed.

"Nice-lookin' cow pony."

"Damn sure oughta be," Jordan snorted, "considerin' the price he fetched."

Starbuck moved around the gelding, running his hand over the hindquarters. On the opposite side, he paused, staring at the brand. It was a Circle B, unknown to him, and yet somehow vaguely familiar. Still, he couldn't place it, and after hesitating briefly, he turned back to Jordan.

"Say he cost you top dollar, huh?"

"Bet your dusty butt, he did! Him and them three there"—Jordan jerked his chin at the corral—"set me back pretty near five hundred simoleons."

"Yeah, you're right, that's a little stiff."

Starbuck walked to the corral and leaned down, peering through the log rails. Inside were two sorrels and a chestnut, all built along the lines of westernbred cow ponies. He studied them with a horseman's eye and, unwittingly, found his attention drawn to one of the sorrels. A gelding, it had a blaze face, and for no particular reason, he was again gripped by a sense of familiarity. Yet he shrugged it off, chiding himself.

Sorrel cow ponies with a blaze face was common as dirt. In his lifetime he'd seen hundreds of them, and nothing remarkable enough to distinguish one from the others. All the same, there was something about this particular sorrel . . . it nagged at him . . . something unusual . . .

Then his gaze drifted to the brand, and he stiffened. He stared at it intently—Box Double X—trying to find reason in a rush of instinctive certainty. In his mind's eye, he slowly took the brand apart, mentally shifted the pieces like a jigsaw puzzle, and began refitting them in logical order. His mouth popped open, and understanding came so sudden he felt as though his ears had come unplugged. It was plain as a diamond in a goat's ass!

Someone handy with a running iron had altered the brand. And done it with a crafty eye for detail! The original LX had been converted into ⟨XX⟩ —Box Double X—altered so deftly that no one would give it a second glance. The blaze-faced sorrel was one of Ben Langham's cow ponies! Probably one of the bunch stolen from the Blue Creek camp a month ago. The very day Langham had offered him the job of range detective. It all dovetailed, time and brand and . . .

Suddenly Starbuck remembered the brand on the dun gelding. Turning, he stepped to the horse and examined the brand more closely. Hardly discernible, but apparent upon critical inspection, was a faint difference in the mark. One section inside the Circle B appeared slightly fresher! An expert with a running iron had altered ⟨P⟩ to a perfect ⟨B⟩ . Whoever it was that had doctored the brands was an artist, much slicker than any run-of-the-mill rustler. His handiwork on Ben Langham's LX and Vernon Pryor's ⟨P⟩ would have gone undetected by anyone unfamiliar with the brands. A man had to be looking for it to find it, and even then it was virtually impossible to spot. Starbuck felt a grudging sense of admiration for the phantom horse thief. With a running iron, the bastard was one-of-a-kind.

Yet the discovery immediately posed a regular briar patch of questions. How had these horses gotten from the Panhandle to Kansas? How many times had the animals changed hands? Who sold them to Clute Jordan? Or, if he hadn't bought them, was it possible he'd stolen—?

"Somethin' wrong?"

Jordan's voice brought Starbuck around. The rancher was standing at his shoulder, watching him with a quizzical expression. Before Starbuck could reply, the farrier approached with horseshoe and hammer and a mouthful of nails. Starbuck stepped aside, patting the dun on the rump, and smiled at Jordan.

"Damn nice little cow pony. Wouldn't care to talk a swap, would you?"

"Not on your tintype! Hell, I just bought the critter."

"Never hurts to ask." Starbuck glanced at the dun, kept his voice casual. "Any more where he come from?"

"Christ A'mighty!" Jordan flashed a mouthful of brownish teeth. "You've got an eye for horseflesh, but you'll need more'n that before you start dickerin' with Ben Echhardt."

"Who's Ben Echhardt?"

"Feller what sold me them horses, that's who. Biggest livestock dealer in Dodge, and the goddamnedest crook this side of perdition."

"Pretty slick, is he?"

"Slick!" Jordan crowed. "Hell, that won't cut it, not

by half. Sonovabitch could lie his way out of a locked safe, and that's a plain fact."

"Well, maybe I'll look him up. I'm headin' for Dodge, anyway, and it don't cost nothin' to talk."

"Says you!" Jordan countered. "You start jawbonin' with Echhardt, and before you know it, he's got his hand in your wallet. Take my word for it, where he's concerned . . . talk ain't cheap."

"Guess I'll just have to take my chances."

"Your funeral," Jordan said, one eyebrow lifted in mock concern. " 'Course, if you mean to tangle with Ol' Ben, you'll need to be in fightin' trim."

"Oh?" Starbuck remarked. "You got some ideas on how I'd go about punchin' his ticket?"

"Naw, hell, you already been broke of suckin' eggs. But you shore look like you could use a good feed. Bet you haven't had a home-cooked meal since way back when, have you?"

"Near as I recollect, the last time was mother's milk."

Jordan's beard parted in a whiskery grin. "Know the feelin', Luke! Know it well. How'd you like to stay to supper?"

"You won't have to twist my arm," Starbuck told him, "if you're sure it won't put your wife out."

"Hell, don't fret none about her! 'Course, I oughta warn you aforehand—she's got her bad side."

"Yeah, how's that?"

"Well, she's a good cook, mighty good. But gawddamn, she's a powerful talker, Luke. Powerful! Talk the molars right out of your jawbone."

"Maybe she'll get me in practice for—what's his name?—Echhardt . . . the horse trader."

"Kee-rist! Ain't it the mortal truth. Sonovabitch won't stand a chance once my ol' woman's got you primed. No chance a'tall!"

"Then lead me to her, Clute. Wind her up and let 'er rip!"

Jordan laughed a braying laugh and flung a wave in the general direction of the blacksmith. Then he grabbed the younger man's arm and marched off briskly toward the house. As they walked away, Starbuck glanced over his shoulder, took a last look at the dun gelding. His mouth creased in a faint smile, and his mind raced ahead to Dodge and tomorrow.

To Ben Echhardt.

CHAPTER SIX

Dodge City sweltered under a late-afternoon sun as Starbuck rode into the South Side. It was the peak of the trailing season, and the vice district was jammed with Texans. Upward of a thousand trail-weary men were in town at any given time, and a carnival atmosphere permeated the streets. Saloons and whorehouses and gambling dives had sprouted like weeds in a berry patch, all catering to the rowdy nature of cowhands. A combination of wild women and popskull whiskey quickly separated most of them from a summer's wages.

Starbuck was in no way surprised by the crowds. Though he generally sent trail bosses north with the LX herds, he had come himself the first year Dodge captured the cattle trade. Hammered together out in the middle of nowhere, it had sprung, virtually overnight, from a trading post for buffalo hunters into the rawest boomtown on the western plains. A sprawling, windswept hodgepodge of buildings, the town was neatly divided by the railroad tracks. The vice district, known simply as the South Side, was woollybooger wild. There, the trailhands were allowed to let off steam with no-holds-barred, gunplay excepted.

But at the railroad tracks, locally dubbed the Deadline, all rowdiness ceased. Anyone who attempted to hurrah the town north of the tracks was guaranteed a stiff fine and a night in jail.

The lawmen of Dodge City had always impressed Starbuck. Handy with their fists, and sudden death with a gun, they rigidly enforced the Deadline. Upon crossing the tracks, it was like passing from a three-ring circus into a sedate churchyard. Along Front Street, the dusty plaza gave every appearance of a thriving little metropolis. Down at one end, flanked by a mercantile and several smaller establishments, were the Dodge House, Zimmerman's Hardware, and the Long Branch. Up the other way were a couple of trading companies and the bank, bordered by cafés and shops and varied business places. To the north was the residential section, and outside town vast herds of longhorns were being grazed along the Arkansas River.

It was sort of eerie in a way. Everyone along Front Street conducted themselves in an orderly fashion, and acted as though the South Side simply didn't exist. Starbuck thought it a remarkable yet highly sensible arrangement. The wages of sin on one side of the tracks and the fruits of commerce on the other. With a neutral ribbon of steel in between. To the benefit of all concerned, it worked uncommonly well.

Skirting the train station, Starbuck held the gelding to a walk. His eyes scanned the row of buildings, then suddenly paused. Toward the end of town, near the cattle pens and loading yard, was a livery stable. A sign, emblazoned across the top of the structure, also identified the proprietor as a livestock dealer. After a fifty-mile ride, there was no need for hesitation. He'd thought it through, and he knew exactly how he intended to approach Echhardt. Still at a walk, he angled across the plaza.

Several moments later he dismounted in front of the livery stable and left his horse tied to the hitch rack. Walking through the broad double doors, he paused and inspected the row of stalls on either side of the building. The place was immaculate, filled with a regular rainbow of odors—old leather, hay, and fresh droppings—blended into a pleasant, musk-like aroma. Except for the stalled horses, and a stablehand shoveling manure, the livery appeared deserted. Then a door opened, leading from an office on the left, and a man hurried forward. By the cut of his clothes, and the gold watch chain dangling across his paunch, it seemed unlikely he'd be caught tending stables. He stopped, nodding amiably, thumbs hooked in his vest.

"Afternoon, friend. What can I do for you?"

"I'm lookin' for Ben Echhardt."

"Look no farther," Echhardt beamed. "You've found him."

"Glad to meet you," Starbuck replied. "I'm in the market for a good cow pony. Clute Jordan told me you're the man to see."

Echhardt gave him a keen, sidewise scrutiny. "That the Jordan with a little spread north of the Cimarron?"

"Yeah, same one."

"And he told you to come see me?"

"Sure did, just last night. Why, aren't you in the horse-tradin' business no more?"

"Oh, no, nothing like that! It's just . . . well, Jordan's a real stemwinder . . . called me all sorts of names last time he was here."

Starbuck shrugged. "Guess it come natural, him bein' so tight and all. But he told me you had the best stock in Dodge."

"Now, that's no lie, friend. Anybody who knows

horseflesh deals with Ben Echhardt! Sound horses and a square deal, that's my motto."

Echhardt was a human wrinkle, stout and full-bellied, but with a face like ancient ivory and a disarming smile. Yet there was something of the charlatan about him; his voice had the cadence and broad exaggeration of a man hawking snake-oil liniment from a torch-lit wagon. It was a disconcerting combination, which he used, with great aplomb, to his own advantage.

Starbuck's expression revealed nothing. "Jordan said you talk good, too. But I reckon horses kind of speak for themselves."

"A profound observation, friend! Very profound indeed. Are you buying or trading?"

"Figured on buyin'. Need something that can double up as a cow pony or a packhorse."

"I take it you're a traveling man?"

"Wrangler, by trade," Starbuck informed him. "'Course, sometimes I catch on with a small outfit and have to punch cows. Never hurts your chances to have an extra pony along."

"Shrewd thinking." Echhardt nodded sagely. "Always admired a man that invests in himself."

"Think you've got somethin' that fits the ticket, do you?"

"Oh, you can depend on it, friend. I'm a little low at the moment, but like Jordan told you, Ben Echhardt has the finest livestock in town. Just follow me, corral's out back."

Echhardt led him through the stable to a rear door. Outside there was a large stock pen, built to hold fifty head or more. But today something less than twenty horses stood munching hay scattered on the ground. With an eloquent wave, Echhardt grinned and cast a proud eye over the animals.

"There they are, friend! None better anywhere in Kansas, and you can mark my word."

"Mind if I have a look for myself?"

"Not at all. They're sound as a dollar. Every last one!"

Starbuck crawled through the fence and slowly circled the horses. To all appearances, he was checking confirmation and general condition. Yet his eyes moved constantly, studying brands for any sign of alteration. After a time he reversed direction, completely puzzled. So far as he could determine, there wasn't a horse in the bunch with a brand similar to those used in the Panhandle. Then, a few steps from the fence, something caught his attention. He moved between a blood bay and a roan, talking softly to gentle them, and made a show of examining the roan. All the while, he kept his head lowered, darting hidden glances at the blood bay and a chestnut standing nearby. One carried a Forked Y and the other a Slash Diamond; both brands had been doctored with the same deft touch he'd seen at Clute Jordan's ranch. Still, the original brands, probably a simple Y and an open Diamond, were unknown to him. Though he had no doubt the horses were stolen, his certainty brought to light a whole new element, and complicated matters greatly. It was now apparent that the Panhandle wasn't alone; horses were being stolen from other areas, as well. Taking his time, inspecting the roan's hooves and teeth, he did some fast thinking. In terms of the plan he'd worked out, it really changed nothing. With a little improvising, perhaps he could still snooker Echhardt into a corner.

Walking back to the fence, Starbuck crawled through and stood for a moment studying the horses. Then he pulled out the makings and began rolling a smoke. "How much you askin' for that roan?"

"Fine animal," Echhardt said expansively. "Pick of the litter."

"How much?"

"Hundred and fifty, and worth every penny."

Starbuck struck a match on the fence and lit his cigarette. "Now that I've heard what you're askin', suppose you tell me what you'll take . . . rock bottom."

"Well, since you're a friend of Clute Jordan, I guess I might shave it some. Let's call it a hundred and a quarter, and shake hands on it."

"Too rich for my blood."

"You won't do any better, and that's a fact."

"Maybe." Starbuck nodded, turned to leave. "Been nice talkin' with you."

Echhardt threw up his hands. "Hold on a minute, friend! Let me ask you something—nothing personal, you understand, but it might change your mind. Whereabouts do you call home?"

"Texas." Starbuck took a long drag, exhaled smoke. "But I've rode for outfits all over, and I never heard tell of prices like that. Not for a common workin' horse."

"What about outfits up north—Montana and Wyoming? Ever rode up there?"

"Nope, got better sense. Way I hear it, them fellers get Injun haircuts real regular."

"There's your answer!" Echhardt trumpeted. "You just haven't got the news, have you?"

"What news is that?"

"Why, friend, the Sioux and the Cheyenne and all the rest of those rascals have been whipped! The army herded them onto reservations the year after Custer went under. There's a natural land boom up there, more ranches than you can shake a stick at!"

Starbuck glued a smile on his face. "You're joshin' me."

"No siree, not even a little bit. That's what I'm trying to tell you. Folks up there want good cow ponies, and they're willing to pay the price."

"So? What's that got to do with the price of your roan?"

"Supply and demand!" Echhardt countered. "Why, close to fifty thousand horses will be trailed to the High Plains this summer. *Fifty thousand!* That makes cow ponies scarce as hens' teeth. And it drives up the price everywhere, even Dodge." He gestured toward the horses. "There's your proof! I sell 'em faster than I can get 'em, and no way to keep the pens full."

"The hell you say." Starbuck regarded him evenly, still smiling. "Looks to me like Jordan just waltzed in here and bought himself the cream of the crop. 'Course, the roan's not bad, but the rest of them scrubs wouldn't last the day."

"Think so, huh?" Echhardt leveled a finger at the corral. "See the bay there, and the chestnut next to him?"

"Yeah." Starbuck felt his pulse quicken, took a casual glance at the horses with altered brands. "What about 'em?"

"I got 'em off the best damn trader in these parts, that's what! Fellow by the name of Chub Jones. Only deals in prime horseflesh! And for your information, he's the same one that sold me the bunch Clute Jordan bought."

"That a fact?"

"A mortal fact, friend! Sure as we're standing here."

"Well, I still think Jordan got the better stock. Maybe I'll just wait till this fellow—Jones—brings in another string."

"Don't hold your breath," Echhardt advised. "I won't see Jones for another month or so. He trades somewhere out in New Mexico, and he only brought this bunch in last week." Suddenly he smiled, shook his head. "You're a hard man, but I tell you what. Take your pick—the roan, the bay, whichever one you want—and I'll come down to a hundred and ten. Now, I ask you, is that fair, or is that fair?"

"Thanks all the same." Starbuck hesitated a moment, thoughtful. "You know, I was wonderin' . . . this trader fellow . . . Jones?"

"What about him?"

"You reckon he could use a wrangler?"

"A wrangler!" Echhardt glowered. "How the hell would I know?"

"Never hurts to ask."

"Then ask him yourself."

"Yessir, I would . . . do it in a minute . . . if I knew where to find him."

"Well, friend, I tell you what you do. Climb on board that horse of yours and head west along the Cimarron. Somewhere out around the Colorado line, you'll find Chub Jones's spread, and when you see him . . . tell him . . . just tell him Ben Echhardt thinks you're a prince of a fellow. Not too bright, but a real prince!"

Echhardt stormed off and quickly disappeared through the door of the livery stable. Starbuck ground his cigarette underfoot, then turned and walked to the corral. He leaned across the top of the fence, eyes fixed on the bay and the chestnut. A slow smile tugged at the corner of his mouth.

He had a name and a direction . . . a fresh trail.

CHAPTER SEVEN

The water was steamy-hot. Starbuck lounged back in the tub, submerged to his chin in suds. A cigar jutted from his mouth, and he stared at the ceiling, luxuriating while he considered the clever fellow he'd become. He was feeling peacock-proud, and immensely gratified by the day's events. All in all, he thought he'd at last gotten the hang of the detective business.

Earlier, after leaving the livery stable, Starbuck had taken a room in the Dodge House. The first priority was a bath, and he had ordered a tub and buckets of hot water brought to his room. Then, lolling about in the tub, he'd scalded off an accumulation of sweat and gritty trail dust. Altogether, with the aid of a hog-bristle brush and rank yellow soap, the cleansing process had consumed the better part of an hour. Afterward, the cigar clamped in his teeth, he surrendered himself to the steamy warmth and let his mind drift.

Upon reflection, he concluded that Ben Echhardt was both a disappointment and a veritable gold mine of information. Before reaching Dodge, he would have bet everything that Echhardt was somehow involved with the horse thieves. The notion had been quickly dispelled, however, by Echhardt's candor and garrulous manner. A thief simply didn't run off at the mouth that way!

Yet, with unwitting honesty, the livestock dealer had supplied all the right answers. At first, when Echhardt mentioned the High Plains, Starbuck thought he'd struck paydirt. It made perfect sense. With fifty thousand horses headed north—at sky-high prices— the logical places to look for stolen stock were Montana and Wyoming. Even now, the idea couldn't be written off entirely. Not with great numbers of Panhandle stock still unaccounted for . . . at least in Dodge.

All the same, the place to look was west, along the Cimarron. The instant Echhardt mentioned Chub Jones, the connection was obvious. One man tied to two different strings of stolen horses pretty much spoke for itself. Like Echhardt, he might very well have bought the horses off someone else. But the connection made him a damned fine suspect. The best yet!

With all he'd learned, however, Starbuck was still stumped. The numbers wouldn't jibe, no matter how many times he sorted them out. The best he could calculate, Chub Jones had sold Echhardt between eight and ten head of Panhandle stock. That was nearly a month ago—at a time when more than fifty head had been stolen—which left a lot of horses unaccounted for. Maybe Jones had sold them off piecemeal, in small bunches. On the other hand, maybe he'd bought only a few head—in good faith—from the real thief. It was possible, but somehow it didn't square with the facts. Jones apparently had an eye for livestock, and a slick horse trader didn't buy a few good cow ponies when he could just as easily buy the whole herd. Then there was the matter of the bay and the chestnut, carrying unkown brands but clearly stolen. A new piece to the puzzle, and one that raised even broader questions. Somebody was stealing horses across a wide area, stealing them hand over fist, and it all seemed linked to one man. Chub Jones.

If nothing else was clear, that much, at least, was chiseled in stone. Chub Jones was the man with the answers. The linchpin that would bring it all together.

On the personal side, Starbuck was immensely pleased with himself. The major questions remained unresolved, at least for the moment. But deep down he knew he'd put on a humdinger of a performance for Ben Echhardt. Compared to the way he'd botched things in the Cherokee Nation, it was an absolute masterpiece. Even his interrogation of Clute Jordan—despite a great effort at hoodwinking the rancher—had caused raised eyebrows and lingering suspicion. With Echhardt, however, he'd played a cool hand straight down the line. Apparently practice made perfect, and with a little experience under his belt, he had learned to assume whatever role the situation demanded. Somewhere along the way, he'd also uncovered a taste for guile and craft and the illusion of masquerade. He actually enjoyed it!

Then too, apart from the excitement itself, there was an element he'd sensed only today. Somewhere between Jordan's ranch and Echhardt's livery stable, he had acquired a touch of expertise. Perhaps he wasn't a professional—not yet—but he'd come damn close that afternoon. A Pinkerton couldn't have done any better, and for a homegrown detective, he knew he'd conducted himself with passing skill. He was alert, relying heavily on logic and deduction, and his instinct had never been sharper. The end result was information and leads, the stuff of investigation and hard-nosed detective work. He was proud as punch. Damned if he wasn't!

Puffing on his cigar, Starbuck abruptly warned

himself to go slow. There was nothing wrong with pride, in moderate doses. But he'd known fellows who'd gotten chapped lips from kissing cold mirrors. And he realized he was on the verge of it himself. That wouldn't do when it came time to match wits with Chub Jones. Not by a damnsight! Cocky had got more than one man killed, and out in the wilds of Cimarron country, he'd have to watch his step. One miscue would get him snuffed out faster than a firefly in a sleet storm. Which was a thought worth remembering . . . all the time.

Still, there was no need to let it put a damper on his spirits. He'd earned a celebration, and he meant to treat himself in style. Tonight he would see the elephant . . . tour the South Side, have a few drinks, then maybe a few more. Once his tonsils were oiled, he might even visit a cathouse. Now that he studied on it, he realized it'd been nearly five weeks since he'd had his pole greased. The thought made his teeth hurt, and removed any trace of doubt.

Tonight he'd get his juices jitterated! Let the ladies of negotiable virtue anoint him with love and sap his log and send him off tomorrow with a limber twig and fond memories of warm things in the dark. Jesus Crucified Christ! It sounded too good to wait.

Starbuck bolted out of the tub and doused his cigar in the bath water. He grabbed a towel and dried himself with a sort of sensual urgency. Then he stepped into a fresh pair of pants, shrugged on a clean shirt, and rammed his feet barefoot into his boots. After hitting his hair a few licks, he cinched his gunbelt tight and gathered his hat.

He was whistling when he went out the door.

The South Side was wide open and running wild. As Starbuck crossed the tracks, nightfall was descending on Dodge, and the boardwalks were already packed with carousing trailhands. Directly ahead lay the Lady Gay and the Comique, the favorite watering holes of Texas cowmen. Within easy walking distance, drunk or sober, was a thriving infestation of gaming dens, dance halls, and parlor houses. A rough-and-ready form of free enterprise prevailed in the vice district, perfected to a near science. The idea was to send the Texans back down the trail with sore heads and empty pockets, and the sporting element supplied all the temptation necessary. Wicked women, pandemic games of chance, and enough sneaky pete to ossify even the strongest man's gizzard. It was a bizarre and ribald circus, irresistible.

Starbuck bulled a path across the boardwalk and pushed through the batwing doors of the Comique. A band was blaring away on the upper balcony, and shouting cowhands whirled girls around the dance floor like a gang of acrobatic wrestlers. The bar was lined three deep, with an even more dazzling array of girls mingled among the drinkers. All fluffy curls and heaving breasts, they resembled kewpie dolls decked out in spangles and warpaint. The back bar was a gaudy clutch of bottles, and as Starbuck elbowed his way through the crowd, a lard-gutted Texan keeled over, glass in hand, and toppled to the floor. Stepping across him, Starbuck quickly filled the hole and whacked the counter with the flat of his hand.

"Barkeep! A shot of the good stuff. Without the snake heads!"

One of the bartenders hustled forward with a shotglass and a bottle of rye. He set the glass in front of Starbuck and filled it to the brim. Corking the bottle, he tapped the counter with his finger.

"Dollar a shot; pay as you go."

"Dollar!"

"You said the good stuff."

"Well, it damn sure better be!"

"Best whiskey west of Kansas City."

Starbuck dug in his pocket and pulled out a handful of double eagles. "Not that it matters, but what d'you get for rotgut?"

"Two bits." The barkeep smiled. "Guaranteed to clean your pipes and melt the wax in your ears."

"I believe you!" Starbuck dropped a gold piece on the counter, nodding at the bottle. "Stick to the good stuff, and keep it comin' till I tell you different."

"You're the boss."

The barkeep collected the double eagle and left the bottle. As he walked off, his gaze shifted to a girl standing with a couple of trailhands. He flipped the coin with his thumb, deftly plucked it out of midair, and jerked his chin at Starbuck. The girl glanced along the bar, then gave him a faint nod. With a bright smile, she disengaged herself from the Texans, kissing one and patting the other on the cheek. She strolled off to a chorus of drunken protests.

Starbuck caught the byplay out of the corner of his eye. He jammed the coins into his pocket, ignoring the girl, and hooked one boot over the brass rail. Holding the glass to the light, he studied the amber liquid with a look of constrained eagerness. Then he lowered the glass and took a long sip, savoring the whiskey a moment before he swallowed. His mouth creased in a slow smile.

The girl stopped beside him, placed a hand on his arm. Her lips were muted crimson, eyelids shadowed with kohl, and her cheeks were tinted coral. She dimpled and flashed a gleaming smile.

"Welcome to Dodge, honey! Buy a girl a drink?"

"Not tonight." Starbuck stared into his glass. "Maybe another time."

"What's the matter, cowboy?" Her fingers trickled across his neck. "Got something against girls?"

Starbuck turned, slowly looked her up and down. She wore a skimpy peek-a-boo gown, which accentuated her breasts and long, lissome legs. She was dark and vivacious, with black ringlets piled atop her head, and her eyes held a certain bawdy wisdom. She ran the tip of her tongue across her lips, staring straight at him while he finished the inspection. Starbuck was impressed, tempted, and she knew the look.

"Satisfied with the goods, honeybun?"

"Yeah, real nice . . . but I'm still not buyin' drinks."

"Oooo, c'mon, be a sport!" Her lips curved in a teasing smile. "We could have ourselves some laughs."

"Sure could, and the joke'd be on me."

"On you . . . a joke on you . . . how so?"

"I saw the barkeep give you the nod"—Starbuck shrugged, watching her—"a dollar a shot makes for pretty expensive conversation."

"Well, you're no dimdot, are you?" She simpered, batted her lashes. "But what the hell, honey? A girl's got to make a living!"

"I suppose." Starbuck took a sip of whiskey, considering all the bare flesh spilling out of her peek-a-boo gown. His mouth suddenly went dry, and he cleared his throat. "You know, somethin' occurs to me, if you wouldn't take offense."

"Try me and see."

"After work . . . when you leave here . . . you run right home, do you?"

"You guessed it!" Her voice rippled with laughter. "Home's right upstairs, honey."

"Shucks!" Starbuck feigned a hangdog look. "Wouldn't you know it! And me all set to ask if I could walk you home."

The girl fell silent, still smiling but subjecting him to a frank examination. He was neat, freshly shaven, and smelled of soap. A rarity among men who reeked of cow dung and sweat. Not exactly handsome, but by no means ugly, and he had a sense of humor. Even the way he'd propositioned her was quietly offhanded, and she somehow knew he would treat her gently in bed. All in all, there were worse ways to fill a lonesome night. She'd slept with them, lots of times.

"I guess we could talk about it"—she gave him a minxish smile—"if you don't mind sneaking up the back stairs."

"Just call me Johnny Lightfoot!"

"Well, Johnny, I haven't said yes, not yet, anyway. All I said was . . . we could talk about it."

"I reckon that'll do for openers."

"No, for openers you'll have to buy a bottle of champagne."

"Oh?" Starbuck frowned. "How's that?"

"Because you were right, honey. Conversation is damned expensive in this joint. Either you buy the champagne—and we talk—or I have to keep circulating and hustling drinks. It's a house rule."

She lowered one eyelid in a naughty wink. "A bottle of bubbly and you get me all to yourself."

Starbuck held her gaze a moment. He found something of the imp lurking there, but her look was steadfast, without guile. His mustache lifted in a wide grin, and he nodded. Then he turned and slapped the counter with lightning-like report.

"Bartender! A bottle of bubbly!"

Lamplight spilled over the bed in a cider glow. She lay curled against his body, her head nestled in the hollow of his shoulder. There was little talk, and they lay quietly, drifting on a quenched flame. Her hair, now uncoiled, was like the wings of a raven fanned darkly across the pillow. Her skin, soft and silky-smooth, tingled as his fingers gently stroked her buttocks. After a long while she sighed, twisting around, and looked at him.

"That's not your real name . . . is it?"

"What name?"

"Johnny." She giggled and punched him in the ribs. "Forget the Lightfoot and just tell me about Johnny."

He smiled. "It's Luke . . . Luke Starbuck."

She repeated the name several times to herself. "That's nice. I think it . . . well, somehow . . . it fits you."

"Now that you brought it up, you never told me your name."

"Lisa." She watched his expression. "Lisa Blalock."

"Same song, second verse. Is it real?"

"Well, it's really Elizabeth, but I don't like to be called Betty. So I fudged a little and picked Lisa."

"Pretty name." He paused, straight-faced. "Fits you, too."

"You're a tease! You really are!"

"Guess we're birds of a feather. You just about teased me to death with that little thing of yours."

"The same for me." She uttered a low gloating laugh. "Only yours isn't so little."

"The way I recollect, you had a lot to do with that."

"Luke?" Her voice was husky velvet. "It was good, wasn't it . . . special?"

"Extra special, and that's no lie."

"Maybe we can do it again sometime, hmm?"

"You can bank on it, and that's no lie, either."

"You wouldn't kid an old kidder, would you?"

"No, ma'am, not you." He deliberated a moment.

"I've got some business to tend to, but it won't take too long.",

"Hah! I'll bet it's business . . . monkey business!"

"Yeah, you might say that—'specially if you're talkin' about the right kind of monkeys."

"Sorry, lover, you lost me."

"It'll keep, just a private joke."

"You're full of private jokes . . . and secrets . . . aren't you?"

He stroked her buttocks and smiled a cryptic smile. After a time, when he remained silent, she snuggled closer and let her fingers trickle down his belly. Then she grasped him, gently fondling and caressing, and felt him grow within her hand. Suddenly his arms lifted her and swung her kneeling astraddle him, centered on his hardness. She impaled herself with a whimpering cry of urgency.

CHAPTER EIGHT

The day was bright as new brass, without a cloud in sight. Overhead a hawk floated past on smothered wings, then slowly veered windward of man and horse. A shallow trickle of water ran listlessly through the riverbed, and the flintlike soil, baked hard and yellow by the sun, was spotted with clumps of withered grass. To the west, near the river, were a couple of buildings and a corral. There was no sign of life.

Screened by a cluster of trees, Starbuck squatted on his heels, staring at the buildings. Since early afternoon, he had watched and waited, scouting the ranch of Chub Jones. Now, with sundown approaching, he had a mental inventory of the operation. All the pieces seemed to fit, and the more he'd observed, the greater became his certainty. The search ended here.

The buildings were crude log structures, with a ramshackle look of impermanence. The smaller one, Starbuck had concluded, was Chub Jones's personal dwelling. It was occupied by a lone man, who had appeared briefly not long after the noon hour. The larger building, clearly a bunkhouse, was occupied by four men. Except for trips to the privy, they had remained indoors throughout the afternoon. The corral held fifteen head of horses, exactly two mounts per man, with five spares in reserve, which was adequate for a small working ranch.

Yet this was no working ranch. Grazing south of the river was a herd of slat-ribbed longhorns, numbering scarcely a hundred head. In this parched land, the cows had to rustle to survive, and from their scrawny condition, it seemed obvious Chub Jones was no cattleman. All the more revealing were the loafers in the bunkhouse. A crew of four hands was about three too many for the size of the operation. The cattle were apparently window-dressing—meant to create the illusion of a small outfit—which unquestionably placed the men in another line of work. The stark isolation of the ranch merely confirmed the thought. A hundred miles from Dodge, out in the wilds of Cimarron country, it was a desolate land of no value to anyone—except to a man with something to hide.

Still, for all its barren solitude, the ranch had a strategic value of no small consequence. To the south, across a lawless strip called No Man's Land, lay the Texas Panhandle. A day and a night of hard riding, roughly a hundred miles as the crow flies, would strike the very heart of Ben Langham's spread. In between, there was virtually no human habitation, nor were there any lawmen. It all seemed fashioned by the hand of God for the benefit of horse thieves.

Starbuck found it ironic that he'd come very near full circle. If he was right about Chub Jones—and deep in his gut he knew it was so—then he had ridden not on a search, but on a fool's errand. The man he sought was practically within spitting distance . . . the whole time . . . the whole damned time!

Starbuck waited until sundown, then rose and stretched his legs. In the distance, there was activity in front of the bunkhouse, and he knew the men were washing up for supper. Unless he was mistaken, Chub Jones would join them shortly, and from where Starbuck stood, he estimated it was a ten-minute walk to the ranch yard. With nightfall approaching and supper on the table, he figured the timing was damn near perfect. All he had to do was act the part.

Before leaving Dodge, he had changed back into the clothes he'd worn for almost six weeks. Three days on the trail had added stubble to his jawline, and earlier in the afternoon he had dabbed a little cow dung under his armpits. He looked grungy and trailworn, and smelled ripe as a billy goat. Which was a normal condition for any diehard saddle tramp. All that remained was his horse.

It was a trick widely known among cowhands, especially the lazy ones. He jerked a hair from the gelding's mane, then knelt beside the near front leg and took a couple of turns around the small pastern bone. He pulled the horsehair tight, tied it off in a square knot, and clipped the loose ends with his pocketknife. Undetectable, it would do no harm, yet it made any animal appear lame. When he gathered the reins and moved off a few steps, the gelding limped along, gingerly favoring the leg. Satisfied, he led the horse out of the trees and proceeded toward the buildings at a slow walk.

Dusk had fallen when Starbuck angled away from the river and skirted the corral. There were now five men gathered outside the bunkhouse, and they watched with wooden expressions, eyes like bullets, as he crossed the yard. When he halted, the gelding hobbled a couple of steps closer and stopped, standing with the game leg crooked, slightly off the ground. None of the men moved or spoke, and after a moment he nodded.

"Evenin'. The boss around?"

A chunky man, squat as a beer keg, separated from the others. He had the look of a bright pig, with wide nostrils, pudgy jowls, and small, beady eyes. In the dim light he squinted, mouth hooked in a frown.

"Do somethin' for you?"

"All depends. You the boss?"

"I own the land, whichever direction you care to spit. That good enough?"

"Yessir, it shore is Mr. ———?"

"Jones." The beady eyes examined him as though he were something that had fallen out of a tree. "L. C. Jones."

"Well, Mr. Jones, I've plumb walked my butt off, and I don't mind tellin' you"—Starbuck gestured toward a spill of lamplight from the doorway—"I was tickled pink when I saw this place all lit up. What with dark comin' on, and a stove-up horse, it shore was a pretty sight."

Jones ignored the hint. "How long's he been favorin' that leg?"

"Since about noontime. I figure he got himself a stone bruise, but hell's bells, I wasn't partial to stoppin' the night. See, all I'm packin' is a little cornmeal and some coffee."

A swarm of flies buzzed around Starbuck's armpits, looking interested. Jones fixed him with a dour stare, and when he spoke, his voice was rough, insistent.

"Mister, we're sorta off the beaten path. How'd you know where to find this place?"

"I asked." Starbuck kept his gaze level, and cool. "Last place I stopped—maybe twenty miles downriver—fellow's name was McKittrick. Never hurts to ask—not when you're headed into strange country."

"Get a lot of handouts that way, do you?"

"Every cripple does his own dance, Mr. Jones."

Jones's laugh was scratchy, abrasive. "You're an obligin' sort of jasper, ain't you?"

"Just try to go along and get along, that's all."

"Whereabouts you headed, exactly?"

Starbuck sensed a sudden alertness in the other men. The question was bluntly asked, but nonetheless loaded, and there was no leeway for mistakes. The wrong answer would get him killed.

"Well, it's this way," he said evenly, "I'm a wrangler by trade. But I'm sick to death of trail drives in the summer and the Rio Grande in the winter. All I've ever seen is flatlands and flies, and I figure I'm due for a change. Thought I'd try Colorado, have a look-see at them mountains. Hear tell they're mighty pretty."

"Who'd you wrangle for?"

"Ere Flecha," Starbuck replied without hesitation. "Cap'n King's spread. Tight-fisted old bastard works you like a greaser and pays you like one, too."

"You got a name?"

"Starbuck. Luke Starbuck."

There was a moment of silence, then Jones gave him a slow nod. "Awright, Starbuck, you can stay the night. But come mornin', you be on your way— mounted or afoot!—don't make no nevermind to me, you understand?"

"Shore do, and I'm obliged, Mr. Jones. *Mucho gracias.*"

"Cut the Mex talk and get unsaddled." Jones turned and walked toward the bunkhouse. "Grub's on the table."

The bunkroom smelled like a wolf den. But its sparse comforts were no less than Starbuck had expected. On the left, just inside the door, was a commode with a faded mirror, and strewn on the floor was a jumble of warbags, filthy clothes, and weathered gear. A set of double bunks stood end to end along the opposite wall, and a rough-hewn table, flanked by a potbelly stove, occupied the central living area. Beyond the table, at the far end of the room, was a wood cooking stove and shelves packed with canned goods. Since there was no spare bunk, Starbuck had tossed his bedroll in a corner beside the firewood.

Supper was typically overcooked and tasteless. A platter of charred beefsteak, accompanied by beans and spotted-pup rice, had been washed down with coffee thick as mud. The men devoured everything in sight, grunting and belching like a pack of carnivores gorging themselves on a fresh kill. All through the meal they kept one eye on Starbuck, apparently taking their lead from Jones, who ate in ravenous silence at one end of the table. At the other end, with Starbuck seated on his right, the largest man in the crew occasionally paused and wrinkled his nose, as though testing the wind. He was tall and sledge-shouldered, with the lean flanks of a horseman. His features were hard, all rough planes set off by splayed cheekbones and an undershot jaw. He had taken the choice seat with an air of ownership, and when the other men offered no protest, Starbuck had immediately pegged him as the bunkhouse bully. It looked to be an interesting night.

After the table was cleared, someone produced a deck of cards. Apparently a poker game had been in progress throughout the afternoon, and from their remarks, the men were anxious to resume play. The big man, addressed by the others as Tate, was heavy winner for the day, and they jokingly threatened to bust his lucky streak. Starbuck tilted back in his chair, rolling himself a smoke, and watched as the men dug greenbacks and coins from their pockets. So far, no one had spoken to him or acknowledged his presence at the table. Yet he had a hunch it wouldn't be long.

"What say, Chub?" Tate stared the length of the table with a crooked grin. "You gonna rathole or take the plunge?"

"Well, I'll tell you, Sam"—Jones fished a wad of bills from his pocket—"I think I'll just sit in and show the boys how to clean your plow."

"Fat chance!" Tate laughed. "Comes to cards, you'll wind up suckin' hind tit like ever'body else."

"Ain't but one way to find out. Quit runnin' your tongue and deal 'em."

Starbuck sensed a rivalry between the two men. Tate probably kept the crew in line and performed Jones's dirty work, but the fat man clearly had a tiger by the tail. It appeared to be a case of brains needing brawn—and vice versa—with ill-concealed antagonism on both sides. A glimmer of an idea popped into Starbuck's head, one ripe with possibilities. Before he could pursue it further, Tate's voice intruded and he looked up to find himself riveted by a churlish stare.

"How about it, shitkicker? Wanna take a hand?"

Starbuck regarded him with great calmness. "You talkin' to me?"

"Ain't nobody else in here that smells like bearbait! Jesus, I like to puked my supper just sittin' aside you."

"The way you wolfed it down, I never would've guessed you had a sensitive sniffer."

"Don't push your luck," Tate muttered. "You wanna sit in or not?"

Starbuck studied his cigarette as though he'd never seen one. A moment passed, and some inner voice told him to follow his instinct. It might very well turn the trick, but if he was wrong . . .

"You know, my daddy taught me a couple of lessons about the game of poker. First off, he said a man oughn't to never play with a light poke, and right now, mine's flatter'n a pancake. Then he told me a Gospel truth, regular commandment. Only a damnfool plays with strangers."

The statement froze everyone at the table. Tate glared at him with a bulldog scowl, jaws knotted tight. Then he gently placed the cards on the table, and when he spoke, his lips barely moved.

"You tryin' to say this ain't a straight game?"

"I reckon it was more on the order of an observation."

"Cut the bullshit! Was you or wasn't you?"

Starbuck smiled. "Take it any way you please."

Tate kicked his chair back and stood. "On your feet, peckerhead!" He spat on his hands and briskly rubbed them together. "I'm gonna stunt your growth and stomp all over you."

Starbuck flipped his cigarette. The big man dodged sideways, and before he could recover, Starbuck was on his feet. Tate uncorked a haymaker, and Starbuck ducked low, belted him in the gut. It felt like he'd hit a sack of wet sand, and out of nowhere, Tate laid one upside his jaw. The brassy taste of blood filled his mouth, and pinwheeling lights exploded in his head. A left hook sent him reeling backward, his eyebrow split to the bone, and he crashed over the chair. Tate launched a kick and he skittered away, rolling to his knees. On his feet again, he circled, feinted with his shoulder, caught his wind, and gave his head time to clear. Then he bobbed, lowering his guard, and suckered Tate into a sweeping roundhouse. Slipping inside the blow, he struck two splintering punches to the chin. Tate staggered, shook his head like a man who had walked into cobwebs, and Starbuck landed a hard, clubbing right squarely between the eyes. The impact buckled Tate and he rocketed across the room, slammed upright into one of the bunks. He wavered a moment, then his eyes glazed and he slid to the floor. His nose looked like a rotten apple and blood seeped down over his jaws. He was out cold.

"Well I'll be jiggered!"

One of the men at the table rose for a better look and Starbuck's reaction was sheer reflex. He spun, crouched low, and the Colt appeared in his hand. The men went still as stone, eyes like saucers. An instant of tomblike silence slipped past. Then he wiggled the tip of the barrel.

"You're the unfriendliest bunch of bastards I ever run across. Now just shuck them guns over here—one at a time!—and I'll be on my way."

"Hold on a minute!"

Jones started out of his chair, quickly sat down when the pistol snout swung in his direction. Starbuck smiled without warmth.

"Mr. Jones, I'll have to borrow one of your horses. All things considered, I figure it's an even swap."

"Look here, whyn't you simmer down and let's talk? You got no fight with me."

"Yeah, and I got nothin' to talk about either."

"Never know." Jones gave him a crafty smile. "You're ridin' the grubline and I got use of an extra hand. Might just make ourselves a deal."

Starbuck regarded him with a cool look of appraisal. "Why would you offer me work?"

"You said you was a wrangler, didn't you?"

"Hell, you haven't got horses enough for a wrangler, and we both know it."

"Forget the horses! There's other reasons."

"Try me."

"I like a man that's sudden, and you're fast . . . damned fast!"

"Hold 'er right there." Starbuck jerked his chin toward the bunks. "Are you talkin' about that pile of dog meat?"

"Damn right!" Jones grinned. "Anybody that can haul Sam Tate's ashes is my kinda man. Havin' you around might keep him on his toes. Ain't that right, boys?"

The other men bobbed their heads in unison, beaming wide smiles. Jones sensed a weakening in Starbuck's look, and quickly resumed.

"C'mon, what've you got to lose? Sit down and let's talk! No harm in that, is there?"

Starbuck hesitated a long while. Then he straddled a chair backward still covering them with the Colt. He nodded.

"All right, talk. But no sudden moves! I'll drill the first sonovabitch that takes his hands off that table. Savvy?"

Everyone savvied, and Jones began to talk.

CHAPTER NINE

"Queens bet a dollar."

"Have to raise you five."

"Too rich for my blood."

"Count me out. Somebody else'll have to keep him honest."

"Not me! I'll fold 'em and watch."

"Luke, you shore as hell ain't gonna buy it! There's your five and another five on the queens. I think you're runnin' a sandy."

"Cost you another five to find out."

"By God, I'll take the last raise! Five more says you ain't got beans."

"Forced to call you, Tom."

"Hot damn!" Tom flipped his hole cards. "Read 'em and weep, pardner. Queens and nines!"

"Not enough." Starbuck turned a pair of fours. "Caught a couple in the hole to go with the one on top . . . three fours."

"Jesus Pesus Christ! Ain't there no way to beat you?"

"Outhouse luck, Tom. Caught the case four on the last card."

"Like shit! I'll bet'cha had 'em wired the whole gawddamn time."

Starbuck smiled and raked in the pot. Across the table, Sam Tate gave him a glance that could have drawn blood. The other men merely shook their heads in wonder, watching as he added to the neatly stacked piles of coins and greenbacks. Then Tom, who had lost the pot but won the deal, riffled the cards and called for a cut. Everyone anted a dollar.

For the past week, night and day, a marathon poker game had been in progress. Almost from the outset, Starbuck had enjoyed sporadic winning streaks. When the cards turned sour, he bluffed occasionally but only enough to keep the other men guessing. He was ahead nearly three hundred dollars.

Yet he felt like a man marking time in quicksand. For all his luck at cards, he had gleaned not the slightest scrap of information regarding stolen horses. Instead, he had been subjected to a heavy-handed grilling by the men and Chub Jones, and told so many lies he'd long ago lost track of the truth. It was scarcely the way he'd planned it.

The night he whipped Sam Tate everything had seemed so simple. With a great show of skepticism, he had finally holstered his six-gun and allowed Jones to hire him on as wrangler. The story Jones told was reasonably plausible. The ranch dealt mainly in horses; the cattle were a mere sideline. Periodic buying trips were made to New Mexico; the idea was to buy cheap and sell high after trailing the stock to Dodge. All the men shared in the profits, and except for light chores around the ranch, there was little to do in slack periods. It paid good and the hours were short. A square deal all the way round!

To anyone with common sense—especially horse sense—it was a farfetched tale. Nonetheless, Starbuck appeared to swallow it whole, and even offered a lame apology for pulling a gun. At the time, he thought he'd given a jim-dandy performance, and figured he had everyone convinced. But in short order, it became apparent he had underestimated Chub Jones.

The tip-off was one of attitude. The men shared cooking chores, tended to their own mounts, and occasionally someone remembered to check on the small herd of longhorns. Yet there was never any mention of horse trading. Almost as though it were a forbidden subject, neither Jones nor the men alluded to it after that first night. Instead, they invited him to join the poker game and spent the next few days asking veiled questions about his past. Later, in casual conversation, chance remarks were dropped to verify details. It was a test, plain and simple, and none too tactfully done. Jones apparently liked his style but wasn't wholly convinced he could be trusted.

Starbuck stuck to his original story, embellishing it with a string of fabrications about the Rio Grande and the King Ranch. Within a few days, the questions ceased and he assumed he'd come through with flying colors. Still, despite the abrupt turnabout, there was no mention of horse trading. The men settled down to serious poker—bitching incessantly about Starbuck's winning streak—and he was left in a quandary. To all appearances, there were no immediate plans for a raid. He speculated on the reasons, wondering if Jones worked on some erratic schedule or simply waited for the urge to strike. There was no way to know—or find out—and trying to second-guess a horse thief was like trying to catch smoke. At last, resigned to wait it out, he joined in the spirit of things and began playing cutthroat poker. The bitching rose by several decibels.

On the average, Starbuck folded three hands out of

five. Unless the cards showed early promise, he got out; the end result, whenever he stayed the limit, was that the other players never knew if he'd filled a hand or was simply bluffing. The one exception was Sam Tate. If only he and Tate were left in a game, he raised like a wild man and bluffed on anything . . . and usually won.

Since the night of their fight, Tate had gone out of his way to avoid trouble. He seldom spoke, and though his hostility simmered beneath the surface, he even treated the other men with a certain gruff tolerance. Yet Starbuck wasn't fooled. A bully never forgot or forgave, and one whipping rarely got the job done. To rule the bunkhouse—and enhance himself in Jones's eyes—he had to squash Tate at every opportunity. He accomplished it at the poker table; with stinging regularity, he browbeat Tate into folding whenever they met head-to-head. Oddly enough, a chance presented itself late that afternoon on Tate's deal. The game was stud poker, with two cards dealt. Tate had an ace showing and bet the limit, five dollars. The next man folded, and Starbuck, who had a king on board, immediately raised. The others dropped in turn, and that made it a two-man game. Tate glowered across the table, studying the king for a moment. Then he grunted a coarse laugh.

"Another five says you ain't got 'em wired!"

"Once more," Starbuck observed, peeling off greenbacks. "You stick around and chase another ace and it'll cost you, Tate."

Before Tate could reply, the bunkhouse door opened. Chub Jones stepped through and walked to the table. There was a peculiar glint in his eyes, and his mouth was set in a crooked smile. He looked around the table, then chuckled and jerked his thumb toward the door.

"Get your gear and get saddled! We ride at sundown."

Without a word, the men began gathering their money, grinning and exchanging quick glances as they trooped out the door. But Tate held his seat, glaring at Jones, hands spread wide on the table.

"Chub, I mean to finish this hand. He's tryin' to buy it, and I've got him beat!"

"Whose bet?"

"Mine," Tate answered. "He just raised."

Jones took in the cards at a glance. "Then call him or fold . . . on the cards you got."

"Wait a goddamn—"

"That's it! Play it like it lays, or you don't play it at all."

"Suits me," Starbuck noted. "Put up or shut up, huh, Tate?"

"There's your raise!" Tate slammed a bill on the table and turned his hole card. "Ace with a ten kicker. Got'cha high-carded!"

"Other way round." Starbuck turned an ace. "I've got one too . . . with a king kicker."

Tate stared at the cards for a long while, then shoved his chair aside and lumbered toward the door. At the last moment, he turned, face wreathed in anger, and scowled at Jones.

"You take him along and you've got mush between your ears! You hear me, Chub?"

"That's up to me, ain't it? You just get saddled and be ready to ride."

Tate stormed out the door, and there was a lengthy silence before Jones looked around. He shook his head, eyeing Starbuck with mild wonder. "You believe in pushin' a man to the wall, don't you?"

"Hell!" Starbuck gave him a brash smile and stood.

"You put Tate's brains in a jaybird and the sonova-bitch would fly backward."

"Maybe he ain't so bright, but he's mean. You keep on pushin' and he's liable to backshoot you some night."

"I sleep real light." Starbuck grinned. "Anybody tries that and I'll put a leak in his ticker."

"Yeah, I reckon you would at that."

There was a moment of deliberation while Jones studied him. Then the fat man pursed his lips, thumbs hooked in his belt. "Guess it's time you and me had ourselves a little talk."

"You're the boss."

Jones nodded, went on. "Been watchin' you, and I like the way you handle yourself. Seems to me you'd fit in real well with our operation."

"Funny thing, I had the notion you'd already hired me."

"Let's just say you've been on trial the last week."

"Well, I guess I must've passed muster, huh?"

"So far," Jones agreed. " 'Course, if you're of a mind, you can still walk."

Starbuck shrugged. "Why would I walk?"

"Some men would." Jones paused, watching him carefully. "See, things ain't exactly the way I told you. We're in what some folks might call a risky business."

"Oh, what's that?"

"Stealin' horses."

The words were bluntly spoken, almost a challenge. Starbuck stared at him blank-eyed, aware that his re-action was yet another test. A lightning calculation warned him not to play the fool. At length, with a canny look of regard, he laughed.

"Had a hunch you were stringin' me!"

"That a fact?"

"Yessir, the whole damn time I kept tellin' myself it smelled fishy. That's gospel fact."

"But you stuck around anyway?"

"Say, look here, there's no angel wings waitin' on me!"

"Then you've got no bones about horse-stealin', that it?"

"Not to speak of." Starbuck abruptly turned sober. "Naturally, it'd depend on the dinero. I damn sure wouldn't risk gettin' hung for wages."

"Naturally." Jones appeared to relax. "We split it half for me and even shares for the crew. How's that sound?"

"Beats the buckwheat out of thirty a month and food!"

"Good!" Jones bobbed his head. "Thought I had you pegged right."

"Lucky for me, too, wasn't it?"

"How's that?"

Starbuck lifted one eyebrow. "How far would I've got if I'd walked?"

Jones glanced at the door. His expression was thoughtful, almost as though he were estimating distance. Then he looked around and his jowls widened in a jovially menacing smile.

"I judge about ten feet. What d'you think?"

"Chub, I'm thinkin' it would've been a mighty long walk."

"Yeah, it would've, for a fact—all the way to hell!"

CHAPTER TEN

The plains were still under a darkened sky. A gentle breeze whispered through the night and dim starlight bathed the land in an inky haze. Within sight of the house, the horses grazed in a fenced pasture.

Joe Sixkiller ghosted through the tall grass. His movements were deliberate, all sound cushioned by the lush graze, and he stayed downwind of the horses. His approach was agonizingly slow, but necessary. Working so close to the house, he assumed there were dogs. Even a faint whicker from the horses would set off howling and barking, and ruin an entire night's work. He took his time.

As he neared the herd, Joe Sixkiller grunted deep in his chest and began making horse talk. The horses eyed him warily, but held their ground, listening. He stooped, talking softly all the while, and gathered a handful of clover. Crushing it between his fingers, he rose, careful of making any sudden moves, and extended his hand to a roan gelding. The sweet scent brought the horse closer, until it stood before him, nibbling clover as he lulled it with low, muted grunts. His hand stroked the velvety muzzle. Then he leaned forward and breathed softly into the roan's nostrils. The horse snuffled, eyelids fluttering, thoroughly bewitched. Slowly, with gentle hands, he slipped a hackamore over the gelding's head. Then he turned, holding the halter, and walked away. The roan followed, still in a daze, nuzzling his hand.

Along the western edge of the pasture, a section of wire had been cut and removed. Chub Jones and Sam Tate, both armed with shotguns, were stationed beside the fence posts. As Sixkiller led the roan through the opening, they kept their eyes trained on the ranchhouse. Some distance to the rear, Starbuck waited with Tom Webb and Frank Tucker. Starbuck had been assigned to hold the gang's horses; Tucker and Webb were to hold the rustled stock. By the time Sixkiller reached them, the roan was gentled and calm, offering no trouble. Webb attached a lead rope to the halter, then began soothing the horse in a low voice. Without a word, Sixkiller turned and walked back toward the fence.

Off to one side, Starbuck watched with mounting respect for Chub Jones. Every man in the gang handled his assignment with practiced skill, and their teamwork was flawless. It was a professional operation, and small wonder that none of the Panhandle ranchers had ever caught Jones and his men in the act. Joe Sixkiller, a renegade half-breed, had descended from generations of Comanche horse thieves. His craft with animals had been handed down from tribal ancients, and he understood the ways of horses to a degree few white men could comprehend. Among his own people, where horse-stealing was considered a form of commerce, he would have been accorded great honor. But while the old days were gone, his wizardry was nonetheless in demand. Chub Jones had given him work, and restored his pride, and it was all very much to the fat man's credit. With Joe Sixkiller, he had built himself an incomparable band of horse thieves.

Yet there was one element of tonight's job that had Starbuck troubled. The ranch being raided was in Kansas—southwest of Dodge—nowhere near the Texas Panhandlé. In terms of gathering proof about past raids, it was a complete washout. All the more baffling was how Jones intended to dispose of the stolen horses. Even with altered brands, it would be foolhardy to sell them anywhere in Kansas, most especially in Dodge. The alternative, of course, was to sell them elsewhere. But that led to a guessing game, and Starbuck had no taste for conjecture. He decided to leave it for the moment. Time would tell, and meanwhile, he was spectator to a master horse thief at work.

Joe Sixkiller took less than two hours to complete the job. Altogether, he made ten trips into the pasture, without once spooking the horses. Every animal he selected was a gelding, and in prime condition. As he came through the fence for the last time, Jones and Tate followed him to the rear. After everyone was mounted, with each of the men leading two stolen horses, Jones led them due south across the prairie. By false dawn, they struck the Cimarron and rode west for several miles in midstream. At a junction, where three creeks flowed into the river, Jones chose the southerly stream and continued on for another mile. There, almost at the water's edge, he led them onto an old buffalo trail. Ahead lay a wilderness of blackjack thickets and rolling hills.

Waving the other men on, Jones waited and fell in beside Starbuck. He was grinning, and with an eloquent gesture, he indicated the stolen horses.

"Not bad for a night's work, huh?"

"Slickest thing I've ever seen, and that's no lie."

"Hell, you ain't seen nothin' yet!"

"I don't get you."

"We've just started!" Jones said grandly. "We'll hit four spreads before the week's out and wind up with better'n fifty head. What d'you think of that?"

"Tell you the truth, I think it's damn risky raidin' so close to home."

"Well, don't start lookin' over your shoulder. Nobody'll pick up our tracks . . . not the way we come."

"Maybe not, but where the devil you figure on hidin' fifty head? That's a fair bunch of horses!"

"See that rise?" Jones pointed south. "There's a little valley over there, hills on every side. Natural holding ground, and unless you know where it's at, you wouldn't find it in a hundred years."

Starbuck gave him a puzzled look. "Chub, I'm not exactly dense, but I must've missed something. So you stole fifty head—and managed to hide 'em—what the hell you aim to do with 'em? We sure as Christ can't trail 'em back to Kansas!"

Jones smiled. "All in good time. There's ways and there's ways, and, like I said . . . you ain't seen nothin' yet."

"By God, it must be a beaut! It surely must!"

"Pop your eyes out, Luke. Pop 'em clean out of your head!"

Jones laughed and gigged his horse. Several minutes later, once more at the head of the column, he topped the hill and led them into the valley.

Over the next fortnight Starbuck grew increasingly bewildered. After the fourth raid in southern Kansas, the gang had assembled a herd of fifty-two stolen horses. A couple of days were spent in camp, with the men loafing about while the horses grazed across the small valley. Then Jones ordered camp broken one morning at dawn, and the horses were gathered in a trail herd. He led them west, along the Beaver River, into a forgotten land.

No Man's Land.

To Starbuck, it was an unexpected and perplexing turn of events. He kept thinking back to his conversation with Ben Echhardt, the livestock dealer. Echhardt had told him Chub Jones always traded in Dodge City, where cow ponies commanded top price. Then too, Echhardt had indicated that Jones was regular as clockwork, trailing a herd into town once a month, every month. Yet Jones was headed away from Dodge!

In one way, of course, it made perfect sense. Starbuck had suspected all along that these particular horses would never be sold in Kansas. The risk was simply too great. On the other hand, the alternative made no sense whatever. Echhardt had mentioned that Jones traded for horses in New Mexico, and the Beaver River led in that direction. But why would he trail horses to New Mexico and trade them there for another herd? To come out on the deal, he would have to trail the new herd all the way back to Dodge. Considering the time and effort involved—not to mention a butt-busting ride of almost a thousand miles—it was a rough way to make a few extra bucks. Since the original herd was stolen, it was all clear profit, anyway. Why not go ahead and sell them in New Mexico? Why not indeed!

There seemed no reasonable answer. It was like a puzzle with pieces missing, somehow incomplete. Echhardt's statements in no way squared with Jones's actions, yet Starbuck never for an instant believed their destination was New Mexico. That being the case, he was drawn inevitably to a dread, and even more astounding, conclusion. Chub Jones had been aiming all along for No Man's Land.

Starbuck's misgivings were wholly justified. No Man's Land literally belonged to no one. Through a maze of obscure treaties, it was an expanse of raw wilderness forgotten by God and government alike. Separated by Texas and Kansas for a depth of some thirty-five miles, it extended in a narrow strip nearly two hundred miles long. Indian Territory marked its eastern boundary, and its western reaches touched the borders of Colorado and New Mexico. In time, this remote and lawless land had become a sanctuary for killers and renegades of every stripe. Not even U.S. Marshals dared venture into the outlaw stronghold, and in a very real sense, it was a place where Judge Colt ruled supreme. A man on the dodge could find no safer haven, and those who rode the owlhoot retreated there with no fear of pursuit. Yet it was a land to be avoided, for it was a land where predators preyed on their own kind. A land where none survived without a finely whetted instinct for the jugular.

For three days now, Jones had led them ever deeper into the wilds of No Man's Land. Dawn of the fourth day found them camped at the headwaters of a tributary running northwest from the Beaver. Starbuck estimated they were within a day's ride of the New Mexico border. But the last leg of their journey had proved his hunch correct. New Mexico lay due west, and the course Jones had set angled away, toward a point where the Cimarron River joined No Man's Land to Colorado. While they were breaking camp, it occurred to him that Ben Langham's spread lay on a beeline scarcely a hundred miles to the southeast. By now, he told himself, Langham had probably given him up for dead. Almost ten weeks had passed since he rode out, and in many ways it seemed longer, more like a lifetime. As he saddled his horse, glancing around at Jones and Tate and the others, he had a sudden urge to see the LX, to sleep a whole night without one eye open and his nerves on edge. Instead, he mounted and took a position on the flank as the gang hazed the horses toward the Cimarron.

Sometime around noon, Starbuck sensed a change in the men. At first, he thought his mind was playing tricks on him; then he listened closer and knew there was no mistake. A bantering tone had entered their voices, and Jones was even trading barbed quips with Sam Tate. He hadn't the faintest notion as to what prompted the change, but it grew more apparent by the minute. They were laughing and joking, swapping jibes, suddenly frisky as a bunch of colts.

Then they topped a low rise and Chub Jones's prediction almost came true. Starbuck hauled up hard on the reins, slid to a halt. His jaw dropped open and his eyes went round as buttons. Struck speechless, he simply sat and stared.

A creek meandered through a stretch of grassland on the prairie below. Willowy cottonwoods lined the stream, and tendrils of smoke drifted skyward through the trees. At a quick glance, Starbuck estimated there were upward of twenty men camped beneath the cottonwoods. But it was the horses that transfixed him. There were three herds, guarded closely by outriders and bunched separately across the prairie. A nose count was unnecessary.

All three herds were uniform in size, each numbering at least fifty head. By no mere coincidence, it was

almost the exact number being trailed into camp by
Chub Jones. Starbuck suddenly grasped the meaning,
and his jaw dropped a notch lower.

He was gazing upon a trade fair of horse thieves.

CHAPTER ELEVEN

"Luke, this here's Monty Hall."

"Howdy."

Hall ignored them. He sat, puffing on his pipe, propped up against the base of a cottonwood. The other men merely watched, their eyes flicking from Chub Jones to Hall. Upon entering camp, Jones had been greeted with catcalls and crude humor from the outlaws. Waving them off, he'd laughed and shaken hands with a couple of men. But while Starbuck was at his side, he hadn't introduced anyone until they stopped before Monty Hall. Now, with an air of suppressed amusement, the men waited as the silence stretched and Hall continued to puff his pipe. Jones shifted to the other foot.

"Goddamn, Monty, you ain't being very sociable."

"Hey, lardass!" one of the men called. "Pucker up and give him a big kiss. Maybe that'll help."

"Yeah, Chub!" another yelled. "Sweet-talk the ole fart! Tell him you're sorry and it won't never happen again."

Starbuck was still in a mild state of shock. His expression betrayed nothing, but he was growing more confused by the moment. The men were a rough lot, and despite their noisy vitality, he knew he'd stumbled upon a pack of hardcases and killers. Yet he couldn't figure Monty Hall. On the sundown side of fifty, Hall was a boozy husk of a man. He was toothless, with rheumy eyes and the constipated look of an oldster past his prime. He seemed totally out of place among these men—a lame dog running with hungry wolves.

Nor could Starbuck figure Jones. The fat man appeared sheepish, almost apologetic. Which was not only damned strange, but curiously out of character. At length, shifting from foot to foot, Jones sighed heavily.

"C'mon now, Monty! You got no call to stiff me that way."

"Humph!" Hall fixed him with a waspish look. "Took yore own sweet time gettin' here, didn't you?"

"Hell, we ain't all that—"

"Says you! Damn me if you ain't the last one ever' time, ever' goddamn time!"

"Look here, Monty, you know good and well we got a one-day leeway. Always have had!"

"Save yore breath and just tell me how many horses you got."

"Fifty-two head, on the button."

"Jumpin' Jesus! It'll take me till dark to get you done."

"Well, we'll get a quick bite—"

"Pot's empty!" Hall gestured at the cooking fires with his pipe. "You'll just have to wait till supper."

"Hold it right—"

"Godalmightybingo! You act like you forgot what'll happen if we ain't done by mornin'!"

Jones frowned. "No, I ain't forgot."

"Then I'd advise you to get the lead outta yore ass. Nuff said?"

The rebuff brought a chorus of laughter from the watching men. Jones turned away, muttering to himself, and walked toward the edge of the trees. Starbuck followed along, now thoroughly confounded. When they reached the picket line, where their horses were tied, he ducked his chin back at the camp.

"Who the hell's that old coot, anyway?"

"Best goddamn brand artist there is, that's who!"

"Does good work, does he?"

"If he didn't, I would've shot him a long time ago. Shot him deader'n hell!"

Jones mounted and rode off. Some distance away the rest of the gang had milled the stolen horses, holding them on a stretch of prairie. Starbuck swung aboard his gelding and reined sharply around, smiling to himself. The day suddenly seemed filled with promise.

Monty Hall was in a class all by himself. Starbuck realized that the moment they led the first horse to the branding fire. Thick stakes were driven into the ground several feet apart, and laid out beside the fire were lengths of heavy-gauge wire and a lip twist. A wooden bucket, with a rag dauber fastened to a stick, was positioned away from the heat of the fire. After studying the horse's brand—Bar S—Hall selected a piece of wire. His hands worked the metal the way a sculptor fashions clay; with a twist here and a curl there, he shaped one end of the wire into a graceful, but oddly patterned, design. A quick measurement against the old brand apparently satisfied him, and he gave the signal.

The horse was thrown and the men swarmed over him. Within seconds, his legs, front and rear, were lashed to the stakes. Tate held his head eared down, while Webb and Tucker kept his hindquarters from

thrashing. Then Sixkiller stepped in with the twist.
He attached the rope loop to the horse's lower lip, then
began turning the handle like a tourniquet. The pain,
intensifying with every turn, quickly distracted the
horse from all else.

Hall pulled the length of wire, now cherry-red, out
of the fire and stepped forward. With a critical eye,
he positioned the wire and laid it over the old brand.
The smell of burnt hair and scorched flesh filled the
air, and an instant later he moved back, inspecting
his handiwork. As if by magic, a simple S had been
transformed into an $\underset{\leftharpoondown}{8}$.

Grunting to himself, Hall laid the wire aside and
collected the bucket. He stirred the contents, which
appeared thick as axle grease and had the faint odor
of liniment, then returned to the horse. With a quick
stroke of the dauber, he spread a dark, pasty layer
across the new brand. Finished, he nodded to the
men, and walked away. The entire operation had taken
less than five minutes.

Off to one side, Jones and Starbuck had watched
quietly. There was no second chance when altering
a brand, and Jones wanted him to observe a while before lending a hand. As the horse was released, and
choused back to the herd, another was being roped and
led toward the fire. Jones smiled and nudged him in
the ribs with an elbow.

"What'd I tell you? Just blink your eyes and the old
bastard's done give us a perfect Anchor Eight!"

"Damned if he didn't!" Starbuck shook his head in
wonder. "That's some trick with the wire. Only way I
ever saw it done was with a runnin' iron."

"Hell, I told you he's an artist! All the time I been
at this business, I've never had nobody question his
work. Goddamn horses look like they was foaled with
a brand!"

"What's that dope he uses, the stuff in the bucket?"

"Secret recipe," Jones chuckled. "Sonovabitch won't tell nobody the mix! But it's pure magic, and that ain't no bullshit. Heals the brand in a couple of days, and Christ Hisself couldn't tell it'd ever been touched."

Starbuck nodded, kept his voice casual. "Guess that's a real comfort when it comes time to sell 'em."

"Luke, I thought you was swifter'n that. Ain't you caught on yet?"

"Caught on to what?"

"Why, Christ A'mighty, we ain't gonna sell the same horses we stole! We're gonna switch with these other fellers."

"Switch herds?" Starbuck frowned, thoughtful a moment. "What's the idea, you draw straws, do you . . . to see who goes where?"

"Naw, hell!" Jones groaned. "It ain't that simple. You pay attention now, and lemme explain how it works."

The operation, according to Jones, was similar to a game of checkers. Several dozen livestock dealers, spread throughout four states, represented the squares on the board. Once a month, the gangs met with horses stolen from Kansas and Colorado, New Mexico and Texas. After the brands were altered, the herds were switched, but always in a rotating order. In that manner, horses stolen in Kansas were never sold in Colorado twice in a row; with four gangs, operating out of four states, there was a constant mix of rustled stock. To muddy the water further, the order of the raids was also rotated. A gang raided within its own territory every fourth time out, and as a result, local ranchers could never establish any pattern to the raids. Seemingly, the rustlers struck at random, always from a different direction. Yet it was all very methodical, and virtually impossible to defend against.

Warming to the subject, Jones next explained how the checkers game was played out. Upon leaving No Man's Land, each gang was trailing livestock stolen from another state. Upon arriving home, the horses were then split into smaller herds, generally numbering ten head or less. Afterward, these herds were sold to livestock dealers over a widespread area. There were never enough horses in any given bunch to arouse suspicion, and as an added precaution, each of the small herds contained a mix of altered brands. To all appearances, the stock had been acquired by an itinerant horse trader who operated on a shoestring and bought only a few head at a time. In the end, the original four herds, numbering more than two hundred horses, had been split into nearly thirty small bunches and sold across the breadth of four states. The checkerboard effect was complete.

By its very complexity, their method of operation virtually eliminated any chance of being detected. With cow ponies in demand, and livestock dealers crooked as a barrel of snakes, there were no questions asked.

"Hell, it's foolproof!" Jones concluded. "Not one chance in a thousand of gettin' caught."

"You know something, Chub? I'd say the odds were better than that, lots better."

"Told you it'd pop the eyes clean out of your head, didn't I?"

"Yeah, and you weren't lyin', either. I thought I'd seen 'em all, but this one wins hands down."

"Guess you're sort of glad you tied in with us, ain't you?"

"Chub, I wouldn't have missed it for the world. That's a mortal fact!"

Late that night, Starbuck lay in his bedroll, staring

at the sky. Several of the outlaws were still gathered around the campfire, playing cards and spinning windy tales. Off by themselves, Chub Jones and three men were huddled around a bottle of whiskey, talking in low tones. To Starbuck, they had the look of generals hatching a battle plan, and he knew it wasn't far from the mark. Earlier in the evening, by listening more than he talked, he'd learned that the men commanded the other three gangs. He assumed, though it was sheer speculation, that plans were now being laid for the next rendezous in No Man's Land.

Yet all speculation ceased there. He was certain, beyond any vestige of doubt, that Jones and his three cohorts were merely gang leaders. Not the ringleader!

Since noon, Starbuck had sustained one shock after another. There was scarcely any need to conceal his surprise, for Jones had been at some pains to impress him with the magnitude of the operation. But in the process, however unwittingly, Jones had also convinced him of something else. The operation was a marvel of planning and coordination. Even the logistics of it—moving hundreds of horses back and forth throughout four states—fairly boggled the mind. Someone with a genius for organization had brought the concept and the men together. And only because that same genius guided the operation could it have functioned so smoothly, with no hint of its existence, for so long. All of that took brains and audacity, a type of vision not found among ordinary men. Which eliminated Jones and the other gang leaders.

At first, upon riding into camp, Starbuck had been flabbergasted by the sight of so many outlaws and stolen horses gathered together in one spot. Yet it was a chance remark from Monty Hall—a remark that visibly rattled Chub Jones—which had left him thoroughly stumped.

You act like you forgot what'll happen if we ain't done by mornin'!

Jones's troubled reaction was no longer a mystery. Simple observation, combined with all he'd learned, had given Starbuck the last piece to the puzzle. Every outlaw in camp, Jones included, was a hired hand. Somehow, in a way not yet revealed, the entire operation was directed from a distance. By a mastermind of some sort! A man with cunning enough to stay clear until the dirty work was done. A man who took no chances and still managed to walk away with all the marbles.

A man everyone in camp expected tomorrow morning.

CHAPTER TWELVE

A red ball of fire slowly rimmed the horizon. Since dawn, when the men were rousted out of their blankets, the camp had swarmed with activity. A hearty meal was wolfed down—bacon, biscuits and beans, with strong black coffee—which indicated a hard day's ride lay ahead. Then the bedrolls and camp gear were stowed away, and the cooking fires doused. Afterward, the men began drifting toward the picket line, and now, at the crack of sunrise, everyone was busily engaged saddling horses. Camp was struck, and the outlaws were preparing to ride.

Starbuck had spent a restless night. Long before dawn he was awake and alert, waiting. By all logic, he told himself, today had to be the day. Before the sun was high, the gangs would have scattered to the winds, not to regroup for another month. Whoever ran this outfit—the mastermind—wasn't fool enough to allow the likes of Chub Jones to operate without orders and guidance. Then too, there was the money. Somehow the loot had to be split, and there was no safer spot than a remote creek in the wilds of No Man's Land. Considering the amount of money involved, it seemed unlikely the four gang leaders would be trusted to deliver it in another manner. A personal accounting was the only way that made sense, and that meant here and now, today. Apart from the logic of it, there was a gut instinct that wasn't to be discounted. For all the scurry and rush, a sense of waiting hung over the camp. Someone was expected.

Yet, as Starbuck threw a saddle blanket across his horse, he began to have second thoughts. Unless that *someone* appeared pretty damn quick, everyone else would be gone. By the look of things, it was only a matter of minutes before the men would be ordered to mount. Allow another five minutes—ten at the out-side—to get the herds on the trail, and that would end it. So it had to happen soon, or it wouldn't happen at all. Which meant his fancy theory would prove to be so much whiffledust.

Goddamn!

Turning to gather his saddle, Starbuck bent down, one hand on the cantle, the other grasping the horn. Then he halted, listening, struck by an almost op-pressive silence. All talk among the men, the early morning grumbling and cursing, abruptly ceased. The jangle and creak of saddle gear went still, and a dead-ened lull fell over the camp. Out of the corner of his eyes, he caught a flicker of movement, and as he turned, Chub Jones and the other gang leaders hurried back to the campsite. Looking past them, he spotted a horse and rider, coming on at a walk through the cotton-woods. He smiled, nodded once to himself.

The horse was a steel-dust gelding, bright as ivory in the morning sun. The rider wore a slouch hat, fea-tures indistinguishable at a distance, and sat his mount as though he'd been frozen in place and nailed to the saddle. Still at a walk, he rode into the campsite and stepped down. Jones and the others were waiting, and he shook hands all around. There was a moment of conversation, with all the men along the picket line watching. Then the three gang leaders turned away, moving swiftly in the direction of their horses. Jones hung back talking earnestly in a low voice, but the stranger interrupted him with an abrupt gesture. Bobbing his head, Jones smiled and moved off a couple of steps, looking toward the picket line. He lifted his hand, motioning, and yelled out in a commanding tone.

"Hey, there . . . one of you boys . . . Luke! Grab my saddlebags! Get 'em up here, and make it quick!"

Starbuck walked down the line to Jones's horse and collected the saddlebags. The weight in no way surprised him, and he slung them over his shoulder. Then he sauntered off, taking his time, aware that he had the attention of everyone in camp. Common gang members, it seemed, were rarely summoned into the presence of the top dog. He determined to make the most of the opportunity.

As he drew closer, a sudden chill settled over him, left a residue of uneasiness. All his life he'd lived by hunches, and the icy feeling along his spine told him he was looking into the face of death itself. The man beside Jones was tall and strongly built, with a huge head and craggy features and a mouth like the slit of a razor. There was no sign of warmth in his wide, dour face, and the fearsome impact was lessened not at all by the menace in his eyes. Almost chalk-blue, his eyes touched quickly, seemed to leave a man stripped and vulnerable, his secrets laid bare. It was an odd sensation, spooky.

Starbuck halted, unslung the saddlebags from his shoulder. Jones snatched them out of his hand and waved him off, on the verge of turning away. But he held his ground, hopeful of forcing an introduction, and Jones dismissed him with a curt nod.

"That's all, Luke. Thanks."

"Who we got here, Chub?" The pale eyes fixed on Starbuck. "Thought I knew all your men."

"Hell, I'm sorry, Dutch! Clean forgot you two hadn't met."

Jones beamed like a trained bear. "This here's Luke Starbuck. Luke, meet the boss, Dutch Henry Horn."

"Howdy." Starbuck extended his hand. "Pleased to meet you, Mr. Horn."

Horn ignored the hand. "How long you been with Chub?"

"Couple of weeks, maybe a little longer."

"Closer to three," Jones noted quickly. "Good man, Dutch! Took to it like a duck to water."

Horn gave him a short look. "Your memory must be slippin', Chub. Near as I recall, we agreed not to hire any new men."

There was a quiet undercurrent of authority to his words. Jones fidgeted a moment, eyes averted, then offered a lame smile.

"Yeah, you're right, Dutch. Hundred percent right! But men like Luke don't come along ever' day." Jones paused, got no response, then rapidly went on. "I'm tellin' you straight, Dutch. No whichaway about it! He's double wolf on guts and got lots of horse savvy too."

"How so?"

"Well, for one thing, he's a wrangler. Got a natural-born gift with horses, and that ain't no lie."

"What else?"

"He's tough, Dutch. Tougher'n boiled owl!" Jones laughed a nervous laugh. "Goddamn, I wish you could've seen it! Him and Sam Tate got into it, and he come unwound like a buzzsaw. Laid ol' Sam out colder'n a wedge!"

"Figures," Horn observed. "You never could handle Tate, could you?"

"Awww c'mon, Dutch, it ain't that. I just know a good man when I spot one. Hell, you oughta see him with a gun. Talk about sudden!"

"That good, huh?"

"Good as I ever seen," Jones assured him. "Plenty cool, too! Got no more nerves than an undertaker."

"What about it, Starbuck?" Horn looked him over in a mild, abstracted way. "You piss ice water, do you?"

Starbuck regarded him with a level gaze. "I generally manage . . . one way or another."

"Why don't you tell me about it?"

"What's to tell?"

"Pick a peg and go from there. Just for starters, how'd you get so handy with a gun?"

"Shootin' people."

"No bones about it, huh?"

"I sleep pretty good."

"How many men you reckon you've shot?"

"Not includin' Mex and Injuns?"

"Why, do you kill one different than another?"

"No, I guess not. Any man that's worth shootin' is worth killin'."

"Regular widow-maker, aren't you?"

"I never pulled on a man that wasn't askin' for it."

"Seems like lots of folks must've rubbed your fur the wrong way."

"I don't get you."

"Well, Chub says you're a wrangler by trade."

"Yeah?"

"So how come a wrangler's been puttin' leaks in all them people?"

Starbuck smiled. "I suppose that depends on who he's ridin' for."

"You ride for anybody I ever heard of?"

"Cap'n King, mostly. Down on the Rio Grande."

"When he hires the man, he hires the man's gun, that it?"

"Let's just say workin' on the border's not for greenhorns."

"You talkin' about *bandidos?*"

"White or Mex, I guess horse thieves and rustlers all pretty much fit the same pigeonhole."

"You've killed your share, I take it?"

"Enough."

"Doesn't bother you, then . . . switchin' sides?"

"Chub says stealin' horses pays good. All I ever got the other way was a sore butt and holes in my pockets."

"Sounds reasonable." Horn suddenly riveted him with a stare. "How'd you come to drift so far north?"

"Got a case of itchy feet." Starbuck hesitated a moment, then shrugged. "Got fired off a trail drive, too. Had a little trouble with the ramrod."

"Killed him?"

"No, just busted him up pretty bad."

"Let's see, the King spread? That'd be the Broken Arrow R, wouldn't it?"

"Ere Flecha," Starbuck corrected him. "The Cap'n always brands with the arrow straight through the letter. Goddamn near impossible to monkey with it."

"So I've heard."

"Yeah, every now and then some dimdot takes a stab at it. But most of the stock he loses gets sold off down in Old Mexico."

The shadow of a question touched Horn's eyes, then moved on. He nodded with chill dignity.

"I think Chub's right. You've got the makings of a first-class horse thief."

"Don't worry, I'll hold up my end, Mr. Horn."

"See that you do," Horn remarked. "Now, if you don't mind, me and the boys have got a little business to wrap up."

Starbuck turned and saw the other gang leaders waiting several paces away. Chub Jones gave him a hidden wink, and with a brief nod in Horn's direction, he walked off toward the picket line. For the first time, he realized his hands were clammy and a trickle of sweat was running down his backbone. Suddenly he understood why there was an odor of fear about Jones and the other gang leaders.

Dutch Henry Horn was a slick piece of work!

Glancing back, he saw that someone had thrown a saddle blanket on the ground. The men were kneeling down, transferring money from their saddle bags to the blanket, while Horn looked on without expression. Starbuck pondered the name a moment, then decided it was an alias. The "Dutch" part was fitting enough, for the man clearly had German blood in him. Stolid and cold, with a merciless set to his jaw and no trace of compassion in his manner. But the name was too easily bandied about to be real. On the other hand, he was one tricky gent. So perhaps it was the straight goods, after all. Wherever he called home—and where the hell was that?—perhaps he went by an alias there. It was a toss-up, and a whole new puzzle to be considered with care.

One thing, though, was certain. To run Dutch Henry Horn to earth would be no simple task. The interrogation just completed was merely a sample of the man's quick wits and guile. The trap he'd laid about the King Ranch brand had been a lulu. It was smooth as butter and cleverly staged, the work of a man who was one step ahead at every turn. All the more apparent, it indicated the extreme caution he employed in every phase of the operation. His tracks were well covered, there could be no doubt of that. Even the way he'd ridden in at sunrise—after very likely watching the camp all night—showed a fox-like cunning that commanded respect. To track him down and take him off guard was probably an option not even worth considering. But if not that . . . then what?

Chub Jones and his gang presented no great problem. There were several ways they could be nailed and put out of action. The most expedient, of course, was simply to notify the Panhandle ranchers and take Jones unaware at his home base. As for the other gangs, Starbuck already had a glimmer of an idea. It would require planning and stealth, and a rather healthy dose of luck. Nonetheless, it had promise, and given time to arrange the details, he thought it might very well work. But the ringleader himself was another ball of wax entirely. So far as he could determine, the man never left anything to chance. All the pitfalls had been anticipated and eliminated, and that posed a bitch-kitty of a question. A real headscratcher.

How the hell to sucker Dutch Henry Horn?

CHAPTER THIRTEEN

A week later the gang fanned out across Kansas. Chub Jones, accompanied by Starbuck and Tate, drove twelve head into Dodge City. The balance of the herd, trailed farther north by the other men, would be split and sold to livestock dealers in towns along the Smoky Hill River. Everyone was to meet back at the ranch within ten days.

At that time, with the herd sold and a final tally on the proceeds, the men would be paid. In conversation along the trail, Jones estimated Starbuck's share would exceed two hundred fifty dollars. The figure was roughly ten times the monthly wage of a cowhand, and it underscored the point that horse-stealing paid very well, indeed. By simple calculation, Starbuck estimated in turn that Jones's share would reach upward of twelve hundred dollars. Carried a step further, it appeared Dutch Henry Horn would clear double that amount. With four gangs in operation, the ringleader's overall monthly take jumped to ten thousand dollars or more.

To Starbuck, it was a staggering figure. There were

scores of cattlemen who seldom cleared that much in a year. One of them was his boss, Ben Langham.

Yet the amount of money involved was merely an offshoot of the central problem. All the way into Dodge, Starbuck had pondered his next step. Slowly, it had become apparent that he would have to risk everything on a single stroke. There was no practical way to separate the four gangs and eliminate them piecemeal. Nor was it reasonable to believe Dutch Henry Horn could be hunted down and taken by himself. Even now, after puzzling on it for a week, Starbuck was still at a loss as to how he might uncover further information about Horn. The man's name had never once been mentioned; it was almost as though the gang members were leery of raising the topic. So any questions directed to Jones—however tactfully couched—would immediately arouse suspicion . . . which was a danger he simply couldn't chance, not at this point.

All things considered, then, he had no choice. The only workable plan was to lay a trap in No Man's Land. To somehow surprise all four gangs—and Dutch Henry Horn—at next month's rendezvous. It was a bold gamble, but one dictated by the odds. An all-or-nothing proposition, with secrecy the key element. An ambush of sorts.

Having settled on a plan, Starbuck was now confronted with more immediate problems. Approaching Dodge, he was reminded that he had to avoid Ben Echhardt, or risk being exposed. Not quite a month ago, he had obtained Jones's name from the livestock dealer; if he suddenly appeared with Jones and a string of horses, Echhardt was certain to make the connection. Any comment, no matter how casual, would alert Jones and lead to questions about his previous meeting with Echhardt. Questions that would inevitably tip his hand.

To complicate matters further, there was the problem of getting a message to Ben Langham. A letter wouldn't do the job; the nearest post office was three days' ride from the ranch, and all mail was collected on monthly supply trips to town. Yet, somehow, Langham and the other Panhandle ranchers had to be advised of the situation. Only then could they organize, and stand prepared to meet him, in secret, at some designated spot in No Man's Land. The problem, then, was one of hiring someone to act as courier. Someone not only trustworthy, but with experience enough to chart a course across open plains. It was a large order, a matter to be approached quietly, without haste.

On the outskirts of Dodge, Starbuck decided he had to get free of Jones and Tate. He needed time to locate a courier—which would require discreet inquiry—and he also couldn't chance an encounter with Echhardt. All the way around, it was necessary that he shed his companions, for at least a couple of hours. After mulling it over, he concluded the best way was the simplest way. As they circled eastward, toward Echhardt's stock pen, he rode up alongside Jones. With a wave of his hand, he indicated the horses.

"Now that we got 'em here, you don't need me anymore, do you?"

"What d'you mean?"

"Well, I just figured you and Tate could handle it from here."

"We ain't got 'em sold yet!" Jones grumbled. "Don't you wanna see how I dicker for top dollar?"

"Say, listen, I've got faith in you, Chub! Whatever suits you is fair by me."

"Seems like you'd take a little more interest in things. What the hell's your rush, anyway?"

"Oh, let's just say I'm green and full of sap."

Jones frowned. "You ain't talkin' about women, are you?"

"Chub, I haven't been thinkin' about nothing else for the last twenty miles."

"Maybe so, but we're here on business. Time enough for dippin' your wick later."

"Later might be too late! Come sundown, the South Side'll be crawlin' with cowhands."

"So what?"

"So I met this gal last time I was in Dodge. She's a regular wildcat, and if you don't get her early, you don't get her at all."

"Goddamn, you must have some case of stiff pecker."

Starbuck laughed. "Tell you the truth, it's a wonder I made it this far. I'm so horny I'm liable to swell up and burst!"

"Where's this gal of yours hang out?"

"The Comique."

Jones hesitated, finally nodded. "Awright, go ahead and take off. I'll meet you there when I'm done at Echhardt's."

"Chub, you're a real sport. First drink's on me!"

Starbuck gigged his horse and rode off toward the South Side. Jones watched him a moment, then shook his head and glanced around. On the opposite side of the herd, Sam Tate quickly looked away, his mouth set in a dark scowl.

Lisa spotted him the instant he came through the door. She laughed and clapped her hands like an exuberant child. Hurrying forward, she fended off a group of Texans seated at a table and rushed to meet him. Her cheeks were flushed and she took his hands, eyes bright with excitement.

"Luke, you kept your promise!"

"Told you I was a man of my word."

"I know"—her breasts rose and fell with a sigh—
"but you've been gone so long I almost gave you up
for lost."

"Well, it took a little longer than I figured. Went into business with a couple of horse traders."

"And I'll bet you made scads and scads of money."

"Enough to keep you all to myself for the night."

"Oh good!" She hugged him and slipped her arm
around his waist. "I was hoping you'd say that."

Starbuck gave her a squeeze, and signaled a passing
waiter. "A bottle of bubbly for the lady! And make it
quick!"

Lisa led him to a table at the rear of the room. The
saloon was in the midst of an afternoon lull, and they
had a corner to themselves. After the champagne was
served, and they had toasted his return, she began ply-
ing him with questions. Her curiosity was genuine,
seemingly limitless, and she wanted to know everything about his business affairs. Starbuck found it necessary to shade the truth, but he nonetheless told a
convincing tale of wandering the western territories in
search of horses. All the while, with one arm draped
around her chair, he was aware of her hand resting
lightly on his leg and the touch of her knee. Finally,
when he'd answered all her questions, there was a moment's silence. She took a sip of champagne, eyelashes
lowered, then glanced at him over the rim of her glass.

"I guess you won't be staying long?"

"Longer than last time." Starbuck watched her eyes.
"Couple of nights, anyway."

She held his gaze. "I hear the hotel's pretty
crowded."

"Tell you the truth, I was hopin' to get a better offer."

"Oh?"

"Thought maybe you could put me up . . . if it's no bother."

"You mean it, Luke? Honestly?"

"Bet your bottom dollar! I'll even square it with your boss, make it worth his while. How's that sound?"

She squealed and hugged him around the neck.

"Oooo, Sugar, it sounds marvelous! Sweet enough to eat!"

Starbuck detected a note of vulnerability in her voice. It was a cry of loneliness, even more apparent than when he'd seen her last, and he suspected it stemmed from her work. Every night was like the night before, with rough-mannered cowhands squeezing and pawing, exacting their drunken demands for the price of a drink. A saloon girl's life was hard and vulgar, and for those like Lisa, the sensitive ones, it was a bleak existence. Any act of kindness, the slightest consideration, touched deeply and left its imprint. The moment and the man were a bright memory, never forgotten.

Yet, however genuine his own feelings, Starbuck was toying with a new idea. Upon entering the Comique, he'd meant to have a quick drink and then get on about his business. All that was changed by the warmth of her greeting and the look in her eyes. He sensed he could trust her—he knew it with gut certainty—and a sudden thought flashed through his mind. There were few secrets in a town the size of Dodge, and his inquiry regarding a courier was certain to raise speculation. By far, it would be better to enlist a go-between and keep his name out of it altogether. Lisa seemed to him the perfect confederate, all the more so because of their personal arrangement. With her as a buffer, his chances were vastly improved, and any qualms he'd had at first were now dispelled. He was convinced she wouldn't betray him.

All that remained was to sound her out. But there was time for that later, when they were alone. For now, he would enjoy himself and continue ordering champagne and persuading everyone he was out to paint the town red. It fit perfectly with the yarn he'd fed Chub Jones, and so far as Lisa was concerned, no pretense was needed. He remembered the last time, and perhaps fresher still was the surprise he'd felt afterward. He had missed her.

An hour or so later, Jones and Sam Tate entered the Comique. Walking to the rear of the saloon, they found Starbuck in a mellow mood and Lisa giggly, well into their second bottle of champagne. After a round of introductions, Jones and Tate seated themselves at the table. Starbuck was expansive, calling for extra glasses, but the men declined, ordering whiskey, instead.

"By golly, Luke!" Jones cocked one eye at the champagne bottle. "You believe in whole hog or nothin', don't you?"

"Easy come, easy go, Chub. Wine, women"—Starbuck waved toward the brass band on the balcony—"and song! Told you I meant to tie one on!"

"You weren't kiddin', either." Jones lifted his whiskey glass to the girl. " 'Specially about your lady friend! She's a real looker, and then some."

Lisa dimpled. "Why, thank you, Mr. Jones."

"My friends call me Chub."

"Like hell!" Starbuck laughed. "Some of the things they call you aren't fit for a cat to hear."

Jones wagged his head. "Luke, you oughta get pickled more often. Brings out your sense of humor, does for a fact! Ain't that right, Sam?"

Sam Tate flicked a baleful glance at Starbuck. With-in him the effects of the bunkhouse whipping had smoldered for nearly a month, shadowing his every thought. He feared Jones was slowly easing him out as second-in-command of the gang. Far worse, he feared the man who had humiliated him was being groomed to take his place. Now, with his face set in an oxlike expression, he downed his whiskey neat and placed the glass on the table. His gaze shifted to Lisa.

"How 'bout you and me havin' a dance?"

There was a strained silence, then Starbuck smiled. "Sam, I'm afraid you'll have to look elsewhere. She's taken for the night . . . all of it."

"Says you!" Tate grunted. "She works here, don't she?"

"Yeah, she works here all right. No dispute on that score."

"Well, I reckon you'd better just climb down off your high horse, then. 'Cause that means she's gotta dance with any sonovabitch that asks her!"

"Wrong." Starbuck fixed him with a gallows grin. "The only sonovabitch she's got to dance with is the one that gets past me. You feelin' nervy enough to try?"

"I might be!" Tate replied hotly. "You got lucky once, but I figure I can still take the kinks outta your tail!"

"No, you figure I'm drunk enough that you might just get lucky. That's more like it, isn't it?"

"Drunk or sober, you can still be took!"

"Don't bet your life on it," Starbuck told him. "Or if you do, take a deep breath! It'll have to last a long time."

A moment elapsed while the two men stared at one another. Tate's face went ocherous, and little knots bunched tight along his jawbone. Suddenly he stood, kicking his chair away, and walked toward the bar. Lisa let out her breath, and Starbuck smiled, patting her hand.

"Goddamn!" Jones chuckled. "Looked like he had a mouthful of hornets and couldn't find a place to spit!"

"I don't know, Chub," Starbuck said amiably. "Since he's all mouth, he'd be spittin' the rest of his life."

Jones pounded the table, laughing so hard his jowls quivered. Starbuck poured champagne, looking immensely pleased with himself, and Lisa gave him a wan smile. She took the glass, holding it in both hands while she sipped, and her eyes went across the table to Jones. Her smile slowly faded.

Starbuck closed the door to her room and turned the key. It was past midnight, and his head buzzed from the effects of too much champagne. But he was reasonably sober, still quite aware that he had to talk with the girl. Wondering on the best approach, it suddenly occurred to him that the morning might be better. She was no slouch with champagne herself, and it was vital that she have a clear head before they talked. He decided to let it wait until morning.

When he turned, Lisa was standing beside the window. In profile, she appeared distracted, staring without expression into the darkness. He crossed the room, halting behind her, and placed his hands on her shoulders. She lowered her head, nuzzling his hand with her cheek, but continued staring out the window. Her manner left him bemused, and after a long silence, he leaned closer.

"Something wrong?"

She kissed his hand, kept her eyes averted. "Luke, are you in trouble . . . with the law?"

"Where'd you get an idea like that?"

"Your friend—Jones—he's no horse trader."

"What makes you think so?"

"I've seen his kind before, lots of them."

"Sounds like female intuition to me."

"Maybe." She turned, her eyes darkly intense. "But it's true, isn't it?"

"And if it was . . . what then?"

"Oh Luke—damnit!—it's you! Can't you see that? I don't care who you are or what you've done or anything else! It's your friends, Jones and that other animal—!"

"I wouldn't exactly call them friends."

"But they've gotten you mixed up in something dirty, haven't they? Please, Luke . . . trust me . . . don't lie to me! They're outlaws, both of them, aren't they?"

"Yeah, I reckon they are." He paused, underscoring his next words in a low voice. "But I'm not."

"You're not?" She shook her head. "I don't understand."

"You asked me to trust you." He lifted her chin, gave her a searching look. "Let's say I needed help. Would you be willing?"

"Anything, Luke! Anything at all!"

"Suppose I had to get a letter to someone—a long ways off—would you be willing to find me a rider on the q.t. and hire him to deliver it?"

"Yes, of course, you know I would."

"Even if you had to keep my name out of it? All hush-hush and no questions asked?"

"If that's the way you want it . . . yes!"

"Do you know anyone that fits the ticket? Somebody you'd trust to keep his mouth shut?"

"Well, I'm not . . . " She suddenly smiled, eyes bright. "Yes, there's an old buffalo hunter! Everybody calls him Gimpy, because he has a game leg and stinks to high heaven. The other girls tease him a lot, but I've always felt sorry for him. All he wants is a drink and a little conversation . . . and . . . well, you know . . . he's sort of sweet on me."

"You think he'd do it, if I made it worthwhile?"

"He would for me. I know he would! And he'd never breathe a word to anyone."

Several moments slipped past while he studied her face. At length, taking her hand, he led her across the room and seated her on the edge of the bed. Pulling up a chair, he straddled it and sat facing her. Then he took out the makings and began rolling a cigarette.

"You ever hear of a range detective?"

"I've heard talk . . . stories."

"It's a story, all right! Damned long one, leastways where I'm concerned."

She smiled. "We've got all night, Luke."

"Yeah, I guess we do at that."

He lit his cigarette and took a long drag, exhaling slowly. Then he told her everything.

CHAPTER FOURTEEN

A gray shroud lighted the sky at dawn. Chub Jones crested a hill and reined to a halt, briefly surveying the small valley south of the Cimarron. Below, grazing near the far treeline, was a herd of some forty horses. Behind him, hazed along by the gang, were another eight head stolen during the night. He waved the men forward and turned his horse down the slope.

Off to the side, riding flank, Starbuck was grimeyed and thoughtful. For the past week, ranging as far south as Palo Duro Canyon, the gang had struck several outfits in the Panhandle. The Goodnight spread had been hit hardest, with smaller ranchers contributing less than twenty head. One of those was Earl Musgrave, whose land bordered Goodnight's eastern line camps. But the other members of the Cattlemen's Association, including Ben Langham, had been bypassed this time out. While pleased by that aspect of the raids, Starbuck had experienced a sense of frustration throughout the week. To be so close to LX headquarters—at times within an hour's ride—had tempted him greatly. Upon reflection, however, he had decided against contacting Langham. Any attempt to sneak off from the gang, especially during a raid, would have jeopardized the entire operation. With no small effort, he'd stuck to his original plan.

As he rode down the slope, he reminded himself that today was the day for the next step. Some three weeks ago, before he left Dodge, Lisa had arranged for delivery of the first letter to Langham. But now, with the raids completed and the rendezvous forthcoming, it was time for his second message. Based on the schedule Jones had followed last month, he knew the gangs would gather in No Man's Land within the next five or six days. Langham and the Panhandle ranchers had to be alerted, and the timing was critical. If they were to meet him as prearranged, then his letter had to leave Dodge by late tonight. Which meant he'd have to bluff like a bastard before the sun was high.

Once the new bunch of horses was mixed with the herd, the men rode to the campsite and began unsaddling their own mounts. Everyone was tired and hungry, their thoughts on breakfast, and no one noticed that Starbuck merely loosened the cinch on his gelding. A fire was kindled, and within a few minutes coffee had boiled. Starbuck poured himself a cup, then rolled a smoke and watched quietly while the others went about their cooking chores. When he finished his cigarette, he drained the last sip of coffee and tossed the cup beside the fire. Walking to his bedroll, he stripped off his shirt and dropped it on the ground. Then he dug a clean shirt out of his saddlebags and put it on. As he finished buttoning and began stuffing the shirttail into his pants, Jones looked around.

"What's with the fresh duds?"

"Aww, you know how ladies are, Chub. They're partial to a man with a scrubbed look!"

"Ladies?" Jones frowned, eyes narrowed. "What the hell you talkin' about?"

"Women—ring-dang-doo!—what else?"

"Talk sense! There ain't no women around here."

"No, guess not." Starbuck walked back to the fire. "But there's one in Dodge just waitin' for the sight of me."

"You tryin' to pull my leg?"

"Wouldn't think of it."

"Well, if you're thinkin' about going into Dodge, then you'd better think again."

"How's that?"

"Cause you ain't!" Jones exploded. "Judas Priest, in case you forgot, we ain't done tendin' to business yet!"

"I haven't forgot," Starbuck informed him. "Thing is, you don't aim to leave till day after tomorrow, do you?"

"What the samhill's that got to do with anything?"

"Plenty, the way I figure it. No sense sittin' around on my butt when there's better things to do. I'll whip on into Dodge and be back no later than tomorrow night. Where's the harm?"

"We don't work that way, Luke. Ever'body stays on the job till it's done, and then we go to town. Not the other way round."

"Chub, I didn't sign on to be a monk. Once a month might suit you and the boys, but it sort of cramps my style."

"Now, look here"—Jones gave him a lopsided smile—"that gal of yours won't mind waitin'! Whatever you've got, she likes it a lot. I seen that for myself."

"It's me, not her!" Starbuck countered. "Hell, it'll be close to two weeks before we get back, and I just don't see any sense in waitin' that long."

"By God, you stay, Luke! That's that, and let's not hear any more guff about it!"

"Maybe you'd rather I draw my time, Chub."

A stillness settled over the men around the fire. For a time, no one moved, waiting on Chub Jones to react to the challenge. At length, scowling heavily, he shook his head.

"Nobody quits my outfit! You included, Luke."

Starbuck shrugged. "Then I reckon you'll have to bend your rules a little. Like it or lump it, Chub, I aim to go into town."

"You push it and we're just liable to stop you."

"Yeah, I suppose you could try. But I wouldn't if I was you, Chub. It'd sure spoil a beautiful friendship . . . spoil it clean to hell."

Jones watched him carefully, weighing the threat. The silence grew, stretched longer, and for a moment it could have gone either way. Then, spreading his hands, Jones nodded and gave him a wintry smile.

"You're a contrary sonovabitch, ain't you?"

Starbuck laughed. "Only when somebody gets between me and my ring-dang-doo."

"Awright, get the hell outta here! Go on and hump yourself blind in both eyes. But, goddamnit, you be back here no later'n tomorrow night, and I mean it, Luke! You hear me?"

"Screwed, blued and tattooed, Chub. You can count on it."

Several minutes later Starbuck rode out of camp. As he topped the hill, headed north, Jones pursed his lips, thoughtful. Then he glanced across the fire, met Sam Tate's gaze, and nodded.

"Get saddled! I got an errand for you."

Early that evening Starbuck dismounted in front of the Comique. He looped the reins around the hitch rack and slowly inspected the street in both directions. The feeling of being watched was almost palpable, and he knew his instinct hadn't played him false. He'd been followed! Quite likely by Joe Sixkiller, for Jones wouldn't have chanced a miscue, and the Indian was practically invisible day or night. The street appeared normal enough, but the crowds of trailhands would only make Sixkiller's job easier. He cautioned himself to keep a close lookout, and with a last glance around, walked toward the saloon.

Inside, Starbuck moved directly to a clear spot at the end of the bar. Lisa was standing with a Texan at the opposite end, and a moment passed before she happened to look his way. Her eyes widened with surprise, and he crooked a finger, wiggled it in her direction. By the time she detached herself from the cowhand, he'd ordered two drinks and had them waiting on the counter. She stopped beside him, her smile tentative, and touched his arm.

"This isn't a social visit, is it?"

Starbuck beamed a wide grin and put his arm around her waist. "I want you to laugh and act like you're tickled pink to see me. We're probably being watched, so make it good."

"Oh, Luke you're a real sport!" She flashed a dazzling smile and hugged him, lowering her voice. "What's wrong? Are they on to you?"

"No, but we've got to play it damn cagey. Jones got his nose bent out of shape about me comin' into town."

"I'll just follow your lead, then, all right?"

"Good enough. Starbuck toasted her, still grinning, and waited until she'd sipped her drink. "Things are movin' faster than I thought. Any chance you can get hold of your friend tonight?"

"Gimpy?" She cut her eyes to the side. "That's him

down there, the one with the beard. He came in a few minutes before you did."

Starbuck took a casual look. Halfway down the bar, he saw a man in his late forties, with a brushy salt-and-pepper beard and battered features. The man was drinking alone, elbows hooked over the counter. Sipping his own whiskey, Starbuck leaned closer, nuzzled Lisa's ear.

"Here's the way we work it. I can't wait till you get off, and I can't risk anybody seein' you slip him a letter in here. So you'll have to arrange for him to meet me somewhere."

Lisa blinked. "You mean he has to leave tonight?"

"The quicker the better, and even then we'll be cuttin' it mighty close."

"Where should he meet you?"

Starbuck considered it. "Tell you what . . . there's some sort of warehouse at the edge of town——"

"Thompson's Wine and Liquors."

"That's the one . . . we'll meet there . . . in the alley."

"When?"

"Now we've got to get tricky, do a little play-acting. You up to it?"

"Mama always said I belonged on the stage."

"Tonight's your chance," Starbuck said, nodding toward a staircase at the rear of the saloon. "I'll go up to your room and get the letter written. You wait a while . . . act like you're pushin' drinks . . . that'll give you a chance to slip the word to Gimpy. Then pretend you're sneakin' off to meet me."

"You want me to come to the room?"

"Yeah, come there and wait. Shouldn't take more than fifteen minutes for me to duck out the back stairs and get Gimpy squared away. Then we'll come back down here together, and whoever's watching me will think we had ourselves a quickie."

"You know"—Lisa fluttered her lashes—"that's not a bad idea."

"Why rush things? After Gimpy's on the trail, we'll have lots of time . . . the whole night."

"You mean it, Luke? Honest and truly!"

"Yes, ma'am, I surely do. You just put on a convincing performance for whoever's watchin' . . . and later tonight I'll turn you every way but loose!"

"Sugar, the bastard will think he's watching Sara Bernhardt. I guarantee it!"

Starbuck laughed and swatted her on the rump. She gave him a bawdy wink as he stepped away from the bar and walked toward the rear of the room. She waited until he mounted the stairs, then strolled down the bar flirting with trailhands. With no apparent rush, she moved steadily closer to the bearded man.

Some while later, Starbuck paused at the bottom of the stairs behind the Comique. He glanced quickly in both directions, then turned south along the alley. A few minutes' walk brought him to the edge of town, and the warehouse. The alley was dimly lit by the glow of lamplights from the street, and a man waited in the shadows beside the loading platform. He moved closer, halting when he recognized the whiskery face.

"Thanks for comin'." Starbuck put out his hand. "I'm Luke Starbuck."

"Jack Martin." The man shook his hand, smiled. "Folks call me Gimpy, but that's only 'cause they ain't got sense enough to lick grease off a spoon."

"Well, Jack, you're all right in my book. I'm much obliged for that little trip you made down to the Panhandle."

"Weren't nothin'," Martin replied. "Besides, that rancher fella—Langham—he treated me like a king, damed if he didn't! 'Course, he was fit to be tied wonderin' where in tarnation you'd got off to."

"How would you like to visit him again?"

"You got another letter you want carried?"

Starbuck unbuttoned his shirt and extracted an envelope. "Jack, it's worth double what Lisa paid you last time . . . if you can leave tonight."

"No problem," Martin observed. "All I gotta do is bag up some grub and saddle my horse. Be on the trail in a couple of shakes."

"That's the ticket!" Starbuck smiled and handed him the envelope. "Just make sure you get it there by sundown day after tomorrow, agreed?"

"Hell, I'll make it long 'fore that."

"Both you bastards get 'em up—*now goddamnit!*"

Sam Tate stepped around the corner of the warehouse. He eared back the hammer on his pistol and waggled it in their direction. Approaching a few steps closer, he halted and looked them over with a crooked grin.

"Starbuck, you're cute—I'll give you that. But you ain't near cute enough, not by a damnsight!"

"What the hell's the idea of buttin' in, Tate? This here's private business, and you're out of line!"

"Cut the horseshit!" Tate rumbled. "We'll just let Chub decide who's out of line. Now, pass me that envelope . . . nice and easy."

Starbuck wasted no time on alternatives. The decision to kill Tate was made quickly, and without regret. The consequences could be dealt with later, but for now . . .

"You're making a mistake, Tate."

"Close your flytrap and lemme have that goddamn envelope!"

"All right, Jack," Starbuck said with a note of res-
ignation, "give him the letter."

Martin extended the envelope, and Starbuck
laughed a bitter laugh, then shook his head. "Honest
to Christ, Tate! When Chub hears about this, he'll
flat skin your—"

Starbuck's arm moved in mid-sentence. The Colt
appeared in his hand and exploded in a streak of
flame. The heavy slug sent Tate reeling in a strange,
nerveless dance. His knees buckled, the pistol
dropped from his hand, and he collapsed in a heap
on the ground. A faint stench filled the alley as his
bowels voided in death.

Holstering his gun, Starbuck turned. "Jack, I haven't
got time to explain. Are you still with me or not?"

"Hell, I'm game! Lisa says you're square, and that's
good enough—"

"Then hit the trail! Make dust and don't look
back!"

Jack Martin took off at a fast limp and vanished
around the corner of the warehouse. Working swiftly,
Starbuck manhandled the corpse off the ground and
stuffed it underneath the loading platform. A gleam
of metal caught his eye and he kicked the dead man's
gun into a patch of weeds. One last look satisfied him
that all appeared in order. He dusted his hands and
set off at a brisk pace toward the Comique.

CHAPTER FIFTEEN

Starbuck forded the Cimarron late the next afternoon. His expression was solemn, and his thoughts were hardened to indrawn bleakness, focused on the task ahead. He figured it was even money he wouldn't live to see the sun go down.

Once in camp, he knew he would face a kangaroo court. Chub Jones would sit in judgment, with the men drafted as jurors. If the verdict went the wrong way, he had no doubt they would also serve as his executioners. Whipping Sam Tate in a fistfight was one thing. The men could applaud that with brutish amusement. Killing a member of the gang was an altogether different matter. One that struck too close to home. An act that would arouse fear and uncertainty, perhaps vengeance.

At first, Starbuck had considered not mentioning Tate at all. Simply ride into camp and act as though nothing had happened. But he'd quickly discarded the idea. Jones would be all the more suspicious if he appeared, pretending ignorance, and Tate failed to return. Once the doubt was instilled, it would fester and cause even greater suspicion. Which could very easily hamper his freedom of movement when they reached No Man's Land. Far better to get it out into the open, somehow absolve himself of blame. Confront them with rage and indignation—bluster his way through—and convince them he'd killed for no other reason than to save himself. Killed because Sam Tate had forced him to kill . . . in self-defense.

It sounded good, but he wasn't at all sure they would be persuaded. Sundown suddenly seemed ominously near.

A vagrant thought surfaced. As he gained the south bank of the Cimarron, he wondered if he'd seen Lisa for the last time. He hadn't told her about Tate, for fear it would upset her and spoil their night together. In that sense, it had proved a wise decision. Thrilled by their success, she had taken him to bed with a fire and passion that seemed unquenchable, left him sated. Yet now, on the verge of a showdown with Jones, it struck him as odd that she intruded on his thoughts. He questioned the wisdom of dwelling on the future—and Lisa Blalock—at a time when the future itself seemed questionable.

A still greater paradox was why he chose to face Jones at all. Why not simply say the hell with it and cut a beeline for the safety of the LX? Under the circumstances, it made a great deal more sense. The only explanation he could offer himself was one of pride. Stubborn pride and bulldog contempt for quitters. Which seemed the poorest excuse imaginable for getting himself killed. But it was the only one he had, and apparently excuse enough for seeing it through. A man stuck until the job was done.

No alibis accepted.

The sun was low, sheeting the valley with rays of fire, when Starbuck rode into camp. The men fell silent as he dismounted, and he felt their eyes boring into him while he unsaddled. With no word or gesture, he went about his business, ignoring them. Only after he'd hobbled his horse, and left it to graze, did he turn in their direction. Walking to the campfire, he halted across from Jones, and still no one spoke. He hauled out the makings, built himself a smoke, and struck a match on his thumbnail. Then he lit up, took a couple of puffs, and at last fixed Jones with a hard look.

"Sam Tate sends his regrets."

Jones's eyes were flat and guarded. "What's that supposed to mean?"

"It means he won't be ridin' with us anymore."

"Why not?"

"Because I killed him"—Starbuck flicked an ash off his cigarette—"Killed him deader'n a doornail."

Jones exchanged a glance with the men and something unspoken passed among them. Sixkiller shifted to the rear, and the other two held their positions, covering Starbuck from all sides. Several moments elapsed before Jones pursed his lips, nodding.

"I suppose you had your reasons?"

"All the reason I needed."

"Which was?"

"The sonovabitch tried to bushwhack me!"

"No, I don't think so, Luke. I think you killed him for reasons all your own."

Starbuck blinked, as though surprised by the accusation. "Where'd you get a damnfool notion like that?"

"Little bird told me."

"Chub, I don't want you to take it personal, but you're full of shit."

"You callin' me a liar?"

"I'm sayin' you'd better check your paintpots again. Tate braced me out back of the Comique and he had a gun in his hand. Any man does that, he's just plain askin' for it."

"Why would he draw down on you with no reason?"

"No reason!" Starbuck laughed in his face. "Jesus H. Christ! You're the one that told me to watch out for him. You said it yourself . . . he hated my guts . . . he was lookin' to even the score!"

Jones returned his gaze steadily. "What were you doin' out back of the Comique?"

"In case you forgot, Lisa's boss don't like folks to think he's runnin' a whorehouse. Even with an invite, you've got to use the back stairs."

"I don't believe a word of it, Luke. Looks to me like Sam caught you—up to something—and you had to kill him to keep him quiet."

"Listen, fat man"—Starbuck's tone was icy—"you keep on crowdin' me and I'll make your asshole wink."

"Think you could take all of us, do you?"

"No, wouldn't even try. But I'll dust you on both sides before these boys ever clear leather. You know I can do it, Chub, so you'd best think on it before you start the ball rollin'."

Jones regarded him thoughtfully, then shrugged. "One time's good as another. No way, nohow you're gonna walk away clean, Luke! Not after what you done!"

"Bullshit!" Starbuck invested the word with scorn. "If anyone's to blame, it's you!"

"Me!" Jones was astounded. "Just how in the billy hell you figure that?"

"Because, goddamnit . . . you're the one that sicced Tate on me!"

"In a pig's ass!"

"Yeah?" Starbuck jerked his thumb at the men. "Well, let's see if the boys here will bear me out. Tate wouldn't have come into Dodge unless you sent him, would he?"

"Now you hold it right there! I told Sam to keep an eye on you, and by God, that's all I told him!"

"C'mon, that don't make sense! Why would you set him to spy on me?"

Jones gave him a hangdog look. " 'Cause I didn't buy your story about seein' that gal. You gotta admit, it's a helluva long ride for a little poontang!"

"Why would I lie about the girl? Or Tate, for that matter! I could've waltzed in here and told you I never even saw him, and you wouldn't have known the difference, would you?"

"Guess not," Jones conceded. "But it still seems damn funny."

"Well, Chub, you and your double-dealing are what got Tate killed. Christ A'mighty, it was made to order! You should've known he'd try to put me under."

"Awright, so I made a mistake! So what?" Jones suddenly flushed, spread his hands in a lame gesture. "Come right down to it, I reckon there wasn't no love lost between none of us and Tate anyway."

"Maybe so," Starbuck replied grimly, "but you pretty near got me killed, and I don't appreciate it one damn bit."

"It's spilt milk now." Jones averted his eyes, tried to collect himself. "What'd you do with him . . . you know . . . afterward?"

"I lugged him down the alley and hid him out behind a warehouse. Things happened so quick, it was all I could think of to get him away from the Comique."

"Hope nobody puts two and two together. Lots of folks seen him with me the times we was in Dodge."

"Hell, one dead man more or less don't mean nothin' in that town. The law will chalk him off for another juiced-up cowhand that got himself killed. Happens all the time."

"Guess you're right," Jones agreed. "All the same, I think we'll steer clear of Dodge when we go to sell this next bunch."

With the situation reversed, and Jones on the defensive, the other men relaxed. Looking everywhere but at Starbuck, they traded sheepish glances and hunkered down by the fire. Jones seemed at a loss himself, fidgeting uncomfortably under Starbuck's level stare. Finally, when the men busied themselves pouring coffee, Starbuck dismissed the incident with a brusque wave of his hand.

"Chub, I'm willin' to let bygones be bygones, but it seems to me I ought to get something in return for my trouble."

"Yeah, like what?"

"A bigger slice of the pie."

"Listen here, Luke"—Jones shook a finger at him—"You just back off! I made a mistake and I ain't tryin' to weasel out of it, but that don't give you no leave to sandbag me. The split's fair and that's all there is to it!"

"Suppose I wasn't talkin' about our split?"

Jones eyed him warily. "You wanna spell that out?"

"Let's say—just for the sake of argument—I was talkin' about the split with Dutch Henry."

"I'd say somebody must've rung your bell. With a goddamn sledgehammer!"

"Why don't you wait and hear me out? You've got nothin' to lose by listenin', have you?"

"Hell, talk away!" Jones gave him an indulgent smile. "Tell you the truth, I could use a good laugh right about now."

"Well, it's like this," Starbuck began. "All the way into Dodge I had my thinkin' cap on. I kept rememberin' you and them other three jaybirds squatted around that horse blanket countin' out money with both hands. And there was ol' Dutch Henry—all by his lonesome—waitin' to scoop it up and run on back to wherever the hell he came from."

"You just beatin' your gums or have you got a point?"

"Oh, the point's real simple. Unless I'm off the mark, I calculate Dutch Henry got about half the divvy. That left a quarter-share for you, and a quarter to be split up amongst the rest of us."

"So you can count! The split ain't exactly no secret."

"No, I reckon the only secret is where Dutch Henry skedaddles off with half the gravy."

Starbuck's tone was deliberately casual. He'd seen an opening and taken it on the spur of the moment. The reaction he drew was little more than he had expected.

Jones gave him a sharp sidelong look. "Lemme tell you something, Luke. You're a bright fella and you're a handy man to have around. But you're gonna wind up stiff as a board if you start askin' the wrong questions. Dutch Henry don't take kindly to people that get curious about him and his ways."

Starbuck brushed away the warning with a quick gesture. "Forget I asked! Him and his big dark secrets aren't important anyway. The thing I was drivin' at's the split . . . the money."

"Then you make your point, for Chrissakes!"

"Suppose we got our heads together—all four gangs —before Dutch Henry shows at the meet. Take it a step further, and suppose we agreed to hold out for sixty–forty—or maybe even seventy–thirty—in our favor! Hell, he wouldn't have any choice! He's only one man, and without us the whole shebang goes up the flume. He'd have to see it our way!"

"Goddamn!" Jones roared. "You're crazy as a loon!"

"Why?"

" 'Cause me and them other three jaybirds you was talkin' about go back a long way with Dutch. He's the one that put this horse-stealin' operation together, and without him we'd still be robbin' penny-ante banks. Or rustlin' cows and workin' ten times as hard for the same money!"

"That's my point!" Starbuck said earnestly. "You're doin' all the work now, you and your men. Why settle for half?"

"Now look here, Luke! I'm as partial to money as the next man. But I ain't stupid! If I ever raised that idea with them other boys, they'd drill me so full of holes I'd never get the leaks plugged up."

"For a man that's never tried, you sound awful damn sure."

"You just take my word for it. I know them boys, and they don't mess around. Anybody tries to cross Dutch Henry and they'll feed him to the crows. In little pieces!"

"How about you, Chub? Those your sentiments, too?"

"Never mind me! You just stick to business and let me do the talkin'. That way, we'll all live a lot longer."

The exchange proved revealing for both men. In the silence that followed, Chub Jones decided he'd sadly misjudged the younger man, and he congratulated himself on having picked a suitable, if somewhat headstrong, replacement for Sam Tate. For Starbuck, it was a matter of having turned adversity to advantage. Aside from learning details about the gang leaders themselves, he had wormed his way further into Jones's confidence. It was an edge that might very well tip the scales in the days ahead. Jones finally broke the silence, glancing around with a wry look.

"Luke, lemme ask you something. Did you shoot ol' Sam, or did you talk the sonovabitch to death?"

Starbuck laughed. "Chub, I reckon it was a little of both. See, he was listenin' so hard, he never heard the gun go off."

CHAPTER SIXTEEN

"Yessir, boys, it's a mortal fact," Jones told them. "Luke's what you might call *real sudden* with a gun. Ain't that right, Joe?"

Sixkiller nodded solemnly. "Strike like snake."

"Snake, my ass!" Tom Webb hooted. "He's faster'n greased lightnin'! *Zip! Bam!* And it's all over but the prayin'."

The men were sprawled out around the campfire. All four gangs had gathered after supper for the usual session of yarn-spinning and tall tales. It was the highlight of the No Man's Land rendezvous, by now something of a ritual. Normally, the stories centered on some prodigious feat of horse-stealing, and were related with a grand air of braggadocio. But tonight it was Chub Jones and his crew who were doing the bragging. The death of Sam Tate was the talk of the camp, and Starbuck a morbid curiosity that piqued the outlaws' interest. Jones and his older hands were treating it as the stuff of legend, and basking in Starbuck's reflected glory. A glory they themselves were at great pains to extoll with much exaggeration.

"Well, if you wasn't there"—one of the outlaws

eyed Jones with a skeptical frown—"it beats me how you're so sure he's all that sudden."

"You questionin' my word?"

"Nope, never said that. But you done told us Tate had the drop on him."

"Shore as hell did! Had him cold!"

"Then suppose you just explain how he did it. Case you forgot, Tate weren't no slouch with a gun hisself."

"The hand's quicker'n the eye!" Jones chortled. "All you gotta do is blink, and ol' Luke, he'll turn you into dog meat!"

"You make him sound like some sorta magician."

"Bet your balls, he is! Christ, I seen him in action once myself! Ain't that so, Luke?"

Starbuck was seated off to one side, smoking quietly in the shadows. Until now, he hadn't joined in the conversation; all the bragging made him feel uncomfortable, and worse, drew attention to him. Which was perhaps the last thing he wanted tonight. Yet there was no way to avoid Jones's question. All the men were watching him, intent at last on hearing his version of the shootout. He decided to play it for laughs.

"Yeah, Chub's right." A pause for effect, then Starbuck went on. "The night he hired me, we had ourselves a few words, and I felt obliged to put a gun on him. Near as I recollect, he lost about twenty pounds of that lard when he shit his drawers."

Jones's sputtering objection was drowned out by laughter. The men thought it a real knee-slapper, and ridiculed him with a chorus of vulgar jibes. But the one outlaw still wasn't satisfied, and waited until the tomfoolery slacked off.

"I ain't heard nothin' yet," he persisted, "that tells me what happened. How the hell'd you walk away clean when Tate had you dead to rights?"

Starbuck smiled. "Only two men at a time knows

the trick, and one of 'em always ends up with a new bellybutton."

"I don't get you."

"Well, the way it works out, one fella does the trick and the other watches. That's the only way to learn."

"But the one watchin' gets hisself killed!"

"That's exactly what Tate said," Starbuck noted, deadpan. "Pissed him off some proper, too."

Jones roared, stabbing a finger at the outlaw. "You sorry bastard, that'll shut you up! Or would you like him to show you the trick personal?"

Starbuck rose, ground his cigarette underfoot. "Chub, I make it a practice never to show off in public. Specially when the big talker in the crowd aims to step aside and hold my coat." He grinned, glancing around the fire. "Think I'll catch some shut-eye. See you gents in the mornin'."

As Starbuck turned and walked toward his bedroll, the outlaws began ribbing Jones. So far as he was concerned, the man had made a fool of himself, and deserved the mockery. He thought it ironic that Jones's attitude had undergone such a pronounced change. Apparently, in the end, might made right, and despite the circumstances of the killing, only the survivor commanded respect. All the more outlandish was the intent behind Jones's bragging. The gang leader sought to boost his own stature—now that Sam Tate was dead—by heaping kudos on the one who had done the killing. It was comic, almost laughable. A dog rolling in the droppings of another simply to fortify the potency of his own smell.

Once in his bedroll, Starbuck closed his mind to the men around the fire. His thoughts turned to the night ahead, and tomorrow morning. It was the second day of the rendezvous, and late that afternoon Monty Hall had altered the brands on the last of the stolen stock.

At sunrise, the herds would be switched, and as the
gangs prepared to scatter, Dutch Henry Horn would
appear to collect his share of the loot. Between now
and then, Starbuck had to make contact with the Panhandle ranchers, arrange the details and precise timing of the attack. All of which involved sneaking out
of camp during the night and somehow returning undetected. No small order given the wary nature of
men who slept light and kept their pistols close at
hand.

Still, for all the risks entailed, sneaking out of camp
was perhaps the least of Starbuck's worries. As he
closed his eyes, willing himself to catch a brief nap,
his last thought was disquieting. He wondered if Ben
Langham was actually there . . . waiting downstream
. . . *tonight.*

The sky was purest indigo when Starbuck rose from
his blankets. All around him were men snoring, tossing
in their slumber, bedrolls scattered helter-skelter
around the camp. The glow of a waning moon filtered
through the cottonwoods, and the fire was by now a
simmering bed of ashes. Without a sound, he cat-
footed through the camp and vanished deeper into the
darkness.

A shadow, moving from tree to tree, he worked his
way downstream. There were five night guards, one
stationed somewhere below camp and the others riding watch on the horse herds. Nearing the picket line,
where the outlaws' personal mounts were tied, he
paused behind the base of a cottonwood. It was es-
sential that he not spook the horses, and all the more
imperative that he pinpoint the guards' position before
moving farther. He waited, scanning the darkness, the
thud of his heart like a drumbeat in his ears. After
what seemed an interminable length of time, he saw a

spark of light on the opposite side of the creek. A man's face appeared in the flare of a match, quickly snuffed. Then the fiery dot of a cigarette winked orange in the night.

Quiet as a drifting hawk, Starbuck faded north through the trees. Circling wide around the picket line, he again intersected the creek some hundred yards below the guard. There he stopped, listening a moment for any sign of alarm, then hurried on.

An hour later, he rounded a bend in the stream and halted. A massive boulder stood sentinel in the night, marking the spot where he was to meet Ben Langham. Yet there was only silence, the inky stillness of trees bordering the creek. Nothing.

"Don't move or you're dead!"

Several men stepped out of the trees, and Starbuck's heart skipped a beat. Walking forward, their carbines leveled on him, the men approached on a line. Suddenly he recognized one of them, the ambling gait and the massive frame. He laughed.

"Call'em off, Ben! I'll come peaceable."

"Luke? Is that you, Luke?"

"It sure as hell ain't Santy Claus!"

Langham splashed across the creek and embraced him in a great bear hug. "Goddamn, you're a sight for sore eyes! Where the hell you been, anyway? We been waitin' here since sundown. Are them bastards camped upstream, where you said they'd be?"

"Hold off!" Starbuck freed himself, grinning. "Give me a chance to get a word in edgewise."

"Christ A'mighty, boy, talk all you want! It's almost like you come back from the dead. I don't mind tellin' you, though, them letters of yours has kept me on pins and needles." Langham laughed, smote him across the back. "All the same, you're one helluva fine mapmaker! We just followed your drawin' and come here like we had the place tied to a string. Damned if we didn't!"

"Ben, would you just close your mouth for—"

Suddenly there were men swarming all around him. Vernon Pryor began pumping his arm, crowded closely by Oscar Gilchrist, Will Rutledge and Earl Musgrave. Upward of fifty cowhands, many of them from the LX crew, emerged from the trees to watch the reunion. Starbuck was touched by the warmth of their greeting, but he felt pressed for time, his nerves on edge. The night was short, with much still to be accomplished, and a long hike back to the outlaw camp. Finally, when they continued to pepper him with questions, he fended them off, palms upraised.

"Everybody hold it right there!"

The men fell silent, and he nodded. "That's better! Now, I don't mean to cut you short, but I've only got about ten minutes before I have to head back. So let's save the jabber for later and get down to business."

"He's right, boys," Langham added quickly. "We're here to get a job done, and Luke's the only one that knows the layout. Let's tie it off and give him a chance to call the shots."

The other ranchers mumbled agreement, and Starbuck motioned them to a patch of ground lighted by the moon. He knelt, then began scratching in the dirt with a stick. Langham and the others gathered around, watching intently. A pattern took shape in the dirt, and they saw he had drawn a crude sketch of the terrain upstream.

"Here we are." Starbuck jabbed with the stick. "Now, from this point, I judge it to be a couple of miles, maybe a little more, to the camp."

"How do we recognize it," Pryor asked, "without stumbling in blind?"

"By this dogleg." Starbuck tapped the diagram farther upstream. "You come around a sharp bend, then the trees start to get heavier, and you're less than a quarter-mile away."

Langham grunted. "You're figgerin' we ought to come afoot?"

"Only way," Starbuck noted. "Otherwise, they'll hear you and we'll lose any chance of surprise."

"What time you want us there?"

"A little before sunrise. The one I wrote you about —the head dog—that's when he rides into camp. Him and the four gang leaders will get together in the center of the camp"—the stick marked a spot, then moved eastward—"and all the men will be down here at the picket line. That's when we hit 'em."

"What about this?" Rutledge proposed. "Suppose we swing one bunch around to the west and the rest of us come straight up the creek? That way we got 'em boxed between us."

"Too risky, Will. Last time, Dutch Henry rode in from the west, and we've got to assume he'll do it the same way this time out. If you try circlin' the camp, he's liable to spot you and make tracks before we even know he's there."

"That let's that out!" Langham told them. "If there's one sonovabitch I want, it's this Dutch Henry Horn."

"No two ways about it," Starbuck agreed. "We've got to get Horn and the gang leaders, all of 'em. That's the only way we'll end it permanent."

"How, just exactly?" Pryor interjected. "Since you're the only one that knows Horn by sight, we'll need a signal of some sort."

"Yeah, I was comin' to that." Starbuck again poked the diagram. "Vern and Will, you bring most of the boys up the south bank of the creek. Everyone will be saddlin' their horses, and when you open fire,

that'll cause a diversion." The stick leaped the creek.
"Ben, you and Oscar come up the north side with
about ten men. When the shootin' starts, you bust
right into the center of camp and let fly. Nobody will
see you till it's too late."

"But what about the signal?" Gilchrist demanded.
"How'll we know Horn's actually there?"

"Keep your eye on me." Starbuck studied the diagram a moment, looked up. "I'll be down at the picket
line with the men. When Horn rides into camp, I'll
walk up to meet him. That's your signal."

"Jesus Christ!" Langham exploded. "You'll be out
there all by your lonesome! I'd rather see you get
clear before the shootin' commences."

Starbuck smiled. "I've worked it all out in my head,
Ben, and this is the only way that makes sense. Besides, if I haven't told you before, I want Horn as
bad as you do . . . maybe worse."

Several minutes were spent rehashing the plan.
Starbuck drilled them until they were letter-perfect,
satisfying himself there would be no mishap at the
crucial moment. Then he shook hands all around and
trudged off upstream. The men watched in silence,
and at last, when he disappeared into the darkness,
Ben Langham found his voice.

"Boys, he's aces high and all guts. Goddamn if he's
not!"

CHAPTER SEVENTEEN

Dawn broke over the cottonwoods and limmed the camp in a dusky blue halo. Sunrise was still an hour away, and the night damp, strongest at first light, filled the air with a crisp earthen smell. As the bleak sky slowly brightened, the camp stirred to the sounds of men awakening.

Starbuck lay still, listening and alert, but feigning sleep. Since ghosting back into camp, scarcely an hour past, he'd had no trouble staying awake. In his mind's eye, he saw Langham and the others creeping through the trees, cautiously working their way upstream. He waited, stomach knotted with dread, listening for a shout from the night guard. Any sudden commotion, or a warning gunshot, would sound the alarm and alert the camp to danger. But there was nothing, merely another dawn filled with the farting and grumbling of men roused from a weary sleep.

Presently, when he heard the clatter of a coffeepot, Starbuck sat up in his blankets, stretching his arms wide and yawning. Across the way, he saw the night guard feeding sticks to the fire, a galvanized coffeepot balanced on rocks near the flames. From the direction of the picket line, the four horse guards, their vigil over the herds completed, trooped toward the fire. Nearby, Jones rose from his bedroll, buckling on his gunbelt, and nodded.

"Mornin'."

"Mornin', Chub. Sleep good?"

Jones grunted something unintelligible and stepped off into the trees, unbuttoning his pants. He relieved himself, splattering the ground with a steamy spray, and sighed heavily. As he turned, tucking himself away, he suddenly stopped and peered intently through the woods. To the north, obscured by the treeline, a horse and rider moved steadily closer to camp. In the dim light, the rider was indistinguishable, dressed in a dark frock coat and a slouch hat. But the horse, snorting little puffs of smoke, was unmistakable. It was the steel-dust gelding of Dutch Henry Horn.

"Goddamn!" Jones whirled away, fumbling with the buttons on his pants. Hurrying toward the clearing, he motioned to the other gang leaders. "Look sharp, boys! Dutch Henry's here! He's ridin' in right now!"

Starbuck spun around, ignoring the flurry of activity near the campfire. For an instant, he felt a profound sense of admiration. Dutch Henry had completely reversed the pattern of last month, approaching from the north rather than the west, and appearing at dawn instead of full sunrise. It was a cunning stratagem! The mark of a man who kept everyone else off balance, forever stayed a step . . .

With a jolt, Starbuck realized his own plans were now in jeopardy. He'd told Langham and the ranchers to expect Dutch Henry at sunrise! Yet it was barely dawn—an hour earlier than he'd anticipated—and he questioned whether they were even in position to attack. All the more worrisome, his diversionary tactics were now out the window. The outlaws had only begun gathering around the cookfire—not at the picket line saddling horses—which eliminated any chance of separating Horn and the gang leaders from their men. The situation was suddenly topsy-turvy, bassackward to what he'd planned.

Still another problem confronted him. As Horn rode into the clearing, Starbuck realized the ranchers would have no way of identifying the ringleader. There were simply too many men milling about camp to single out one from the others. From a distance, Horn would appear to be one of the crowd, just another horse thief.

His nerves jangled, Starbuck watched as Horn dismounted several yards from the fire. Jones and the other gang leaders, lugging their saddlebags, went to meet him. After a few minutes' conversation, a blanket was spread on the ground and the men began counting out money. Pondering the turn of events, Starbuck knew he had to devise a new plan, and do it quickly. Everything hinged on two elements, vital to the success of any attack. Somehow he must stall for time, delay Horn's departure until the ranchers were in position. Then, at the very last minute, he must somehow identify Horn in a manner unmistakable to Langham and the men north of the creek. Only one way occurred to him, and he swiftly calculated the risk involved. By no means the best of schemes, he nonetheless decided it would have to do. Walking to the fire, he rolled a cigarette, poured himself a cup of coffee, and settled down to wait.

A short time later, Horn and the gang leaders seemed to have concluded their business. The men stepped back, talking among themselves, while Horn knelt and began stuffing the money into his own saddlebags. Starbuck waited until the very last moment, when Horn had the saddlebags strapped in place and turned for a final word with the men. Then he rose, resigned to what he must do, and moved toward them at a deliberate pace.

As he approached, Horn and the men stopped talking. Jones frowned, and the others studied him with a mixture of surprise and irritation. He ignored them, halting a few feet away, staring directly at Horn.

"Dutch Henry, I'd like to have a word with you."

Horn fixed him with a curious look. "What's on your mind?"

"Money." Starbuck dismissed the gang leaders with a wave. "Nothin' against these fellas, but the split's sort of lopsided, and I figured it was time somebody spoke up."

"Holy Jumpin' Jesus!" Jones erupted. "You crazy sonovabitch, you get your ass down there and start saddlin'! I mean right now!"

"Hold it!" Horn ordered. "Let him have his say."

"Dutch, I swear to God I didn't have nothin' to do with this! Whatever he's after, he cooked it up all by hisself. Honest to Christ!"

"It's all right, Chub." Horn turned a cold eye on Starbuck. "You elected yourself to do the talkin' for everybody, that it?"

"Well, it shore didn't appear nobody else would do it."

"Why's that, you reckon?"

" 'Cause they're all scared shitless of you, that's why."

"And you're not?"

"Oh, I'm a little nervy, but I don't scare as easy as some."

"So you took it on yourself to brace me . . . just like that?"

"Only way I know, straight out and get to it!"

"Starbuck," Horn said with wintry malice, "it appears to me you're gettin' too big for your britches."

On the north side of the creek, Ben Langham paused some fifty yards below the camp. Behind him were Oscar Gilchrist and ten cowhands, all armed with carbines. He motioned them to the ground and dropped to one knee beside a cottonwood. Scanning the area ahead, he spotted the picket line, and a short distance upstream, the campsite itself. Smoke drifted skyward from the cooking fire, and through the dusky light it appeared the outlaws were preparing to break camp. He smiled, nodding to himself. Everything was right on schedule, exactly as Starbuck had described it. Perfect.

Then he squinted, looking closer. Off to one side, Starbuck stood facing a small group of men. The discussion appeared heated, and oddly enough, Starbuck and one other man were doing all the talking. Even more puzzling, the man was standing beside a saddled horse, steel-dust in color. It was almost as though Starbuck had caught him before he could mount and ride out of camp.

Or maybe he'd just now ridden into camp!

Langham frowned, considering the only possibility that made sense. The man was Dutch Henry Horn—had to be!—and the other four were the gang leaders. For whatever reason, Horn had arrived in camp before sunrise, upsetting the timetable Starbuck had laid out. Which led to a fearful conclusion. Starbuck was holding him there, stalling for time. To all appearances, he'd provoked an argument with Horn to identify him, single him out from the crowd. But it was a perilous dodge, and it wouldn't last long. Starbuck was playing with dynamite, and he'd already lit the fuse. Time was running out.

Langham rose and signaled his men. He waved his arms, spreading them on a line abreast of him, then motioned toward the camp. At a measured pace, their carbines cocked and ready, they advanced through the trees.

Vernon Pryor and Will Rutledge were huddled behind a tree on the opposite side of the creek. They watched, thoroughly astounded, as Langham led his men forward. From their position, directly opposite the picket line, Starbuck was nowhere in sight. All they could make out was a throng of men milling about the campsite. Yet Langham was moving to attack—long before sunrise!

After a hurried conference, they could only surmise that Langham had received the signal from Starbuck. Nothing else made sense. Whether or not Dutch Henry Horn had arrived in camp was a moot question. But there seemed no doubt that Starbuck, for reasons all his own, had signaled an early attack. Otherwise, Ben Langham would never have jumped the gun.

A long moment ensued as they deliberated their own course of action. The outlaws were even now breaking camp, but it was clear very few of them would reach the picket line before Langham struck from the north. Their choice, then, was to hold their position, taking potshots from a distance, or advance on the camp. With Langham already on the move, it was no choice at all. If the outlaws wouldn't come to them, then they must go to the outlaws.

Pryor climbed to his feet, with Rutledge at his side, and raised his arm. Some forty cowhands emerged from the trees, their carbines at the ready, and stood waiting. Pryor dropped his arm and led them splashing across the creek. On the opposite bank they

fanned out, walking softly through the murk of the
fading dawn. A horse whickered as they neared the
picket line.

"Seems to me," Starbuck observed, "you're a mite
too stingy for your own good."

"If that's a threat," Horn said with a trace of
amusement, "you've got some chore on your hands.
In case you haven't looked around, it's you against
us . . . all of us."

"Maybe, maybe not." Starbuck smiled. "If we was
to put it to a vote, I've got an idea you'd be the one
that comes out on the short end of the stick."

"Got it all figured out, have you?"

"Well, let's just say I think most of the boys would
go along with me."

"Forget it! There's only one vote that counts in this
outfit, and that's the way she stays."

"Hell, Dutch Henry, nothin' stays the same forever.
Sometimes you gotta bend with the wind."

"I don't hear no wind, but I'm sure gettin' tired of
listenin' to a blowhard."

"I'll be damned! You think I'm tryin' to run a
sandy, don't you?"

"No, you're done tryin'," Horn countered. "You've
shot your wad, and all you bought yourself is a peck
of trouble."

"Wanna bet?"

Starbuck turned away, sensing he'd pushed it to the
limit. Horn was through talking, and if he hoped to
stall any longer, it would require a switch in tactics.
Walking off several paces, he halted and raised his
voice in a blustering shout.

"Hey, there! You boys give a listen! Dutch Henry
wants a word with you!"

Chub Jones and the gang leaders stared at him

with slack-jawed amazement. The men themselves, arms loaded with gear as they trooped toward the picket line, wheeled around in surprise. Even Dutch Henry Horn was taken aback, but the shock lasted a mere instant. His eyes hooded and he pulled his gun. Thumbing the hammer, he took deliberate aim, sights centered on Starbuck's shoulder blades.

The metallic whirr of the hammer caught Starbuck unprepared, his arm raised to summon the men. All in a motion, acting on sheer reflex, he threw himself sideways and drew his Colt. But as he hit the ground and rolled, a rifle cracked from the treeline north of the camp. A slug plucked the lapel of Horn's coat, and, whistling past, fried the air around his horse's ears. The horse reared, and Horn grabbed the reins, momentarily shielded from Starbuck's view. Then the gunfire became general, a dozen carbines spitting lead from the cottonwoods.

As though struck by a scythe, the three gang leaders went down in a bunch, dark stains spotting their clothes. Chub Jones, miraculously untouched, had already drawn on Starbuck and snapped a hurried shot. Dirt exploded in Starbuck's face, and he quickly shifted aim, touching off the trigger. Jones was jerked off his feet, hogsheads of blood spurting from his kneecap, and pitched raglike to the ground. Swinging around, Starbuck saw Horn mounted and spurring hard, draped low over his horse's neck. Cursing with rage, Starbuck thumbed off shot after shot, blazing away until the hammer fell on an empty chamber. By then, Horn was deep in the trees, pounding west at a hard gallop.

Starbuck's immediate reaction was to find a horse and give chase. But as he scrambled to his feet, he suddenly became aware of a raging battle to his rear. At the opening shot, the outlaws had flung their gear aside and commenced firing on Langham's men. Then, with devastating volley, the force led by Pryor and Rutledge struck them from the flank. Within a matter of seconds, nearly half the outlaw band was killed outright. Several more were mortally wounded, winnowed to earth by a rolling barrage that swept the clearing. The survivors, out-gunned and out-flanked, quickly called it quits. Tossing their guns to the ground, they raised their arms, and as suddenly as it began, the fight ended.

Langham's men, and the larger group led by Pryor, stepped from the trees and slowly converged on the clearing. Of the original band, numbering upward of twenty outlaws, only five remained standing. The others lay dead or dying, literally cut to shreds by the murderous crossfire. Later Langham would estimate that nearly three hundred rifle slugs had crisscrossed the clearing in less than thirty seconds, and marvel that anyone had lived through the holocaust. But, for now, he motioned his men to take charge of the survivors, and walked toward Starbuck.

After shucking empties from his pistol, Starbuck had reloaded and approached the fallen gang leaders. Three were dead and Chub Jones lay writhing in agony, clutching his shattered kneecap. Starbuck's expression was stoic, and he stood watching blood seep through Jones's fingers, vaguely noting that it puddled a rich chocolate-brown on the earth. As Langham halted beside him, Starbuck holstered his gun and nodded.

"Thanks."

"For what?"

"For gettin' here in time. Somebody saved my bacon with that first shot."

"Some shot!" Langham grumbled. "Clean missed the sonovabitch! I must be gettin' old."

"Close enough to count," Starbuck remarked. "You nicked his coat front, threw him off. I saw the dust fly."

"Close don't count, 'cept in horseshoes. I should've drilled him straight through the lights! Think I'll get myself some specs."

"I'm still obliged. Bastard had me cold, and no two ways about it."

Langham grunted, wiggled his rifle barrel at Jones. "Who we got here?"

"Chub Jones, the one I've been ridin' with."

"You shoot him?"

"Yeah." Starbuck studied on it a moment. "Guess we ought to do somethin' about his leg before he bleeds to death."

"Waste of time!" Langham said curtly. "He ain't gonna live long enough for it to matter."

"You still plannin' to string 'em up?"

"Why, you got a better idea?"

"No, reckon not."

For a time, each man lost in his own thoughts, they fell silent, watching Jones bleed. Then Starbuck turned away and stood gazing west along the creek. His eyes were distant, as though fixed on something visible only to himself, and his mouth was set in a hard line. Langham kicked at the dirt, frowning thoughtfully, and gave him a sidelong glance.

"You thinkin' the same thing I'm thinkin'?"

"Wouldn't be surprised."

"Got any idea where he's headed?"

"No, but I've got a hunch who's gonna tell us."

"Yeah, who's that?"

Starbuck turned just far enough to rivet Jones with a cold look. "Three guesses, and the first two don't count."

CHAPTER EIGHTEEN

The buzzards dropped lower as a mid-morning sun beat down on the cottonwoods. Quartering a sector of sky, the scavengers slowly wheeled and circled over the clearing below. With mindless patience, they waited for the living to relinquish the dead.

Corpses littered the campsite, and a warm breeze was ripe with the stench of death. The outlaws lay where they had fallen, sprawled and grotesque, their bodies stiffening in a welter of dried blood. Under a huge cottonwood, Chub Jones and the five survivors, one of them Joe Sixkiller, sat staring blankly at the carnage. Sixkiller and the others were bound, arms behind their backs, their wrists cinched tight. Jones was unbound but ashen-faced, gritting his teeth against the pain. A tourniquet had staunched the flow of blood from his kneecap, and his leg was stretched flat on the ground. There was no conversation among the men, and for the past couple of hours, like the buzzards overhead, they had waited with grim patience. All of them understood how it would end.

The delay, rather than humane, was strictly a practical measure. After a long night, capped by a savage minute of bloodletting, the attackers needed time to regroup and collect themselves. To their surprise, the cowhands had discovered that killing was hard work and, oddly enough, increased a man's appetite. Once their horses were brought upstream, at Langham's order, the men replenished themselves with cold rations and several gallons of hot coffee. A few were bothered by the corpse-strewn campsite, but for the most part they ate with gusto and swapped grisly recollections of the shootout. While several of them were nursing wounds, only three of their number had been killed, and that alone was cause for celebration. The meal was a welcome respite, and their laughter the quiet laughter of men who had closed with death and emerged alive. Toward the end, however, lingering over a final cup of coffee, their mood turned somber. With the sun high, and the buzzards circling lower, they were reminded of the distasteful part. The job yet to be done.

Off to one side, Starbuck huddled in conversation with Langham and the other ranchers. Their talk centered on Chub Jones, and for once they were in total agreement. Starbuck had proposed a plan, and now, as they nodded approval, he concluded in a flat voice.

"That's the way we'll play it, then. You gents just act natural—like it'd all been settled beforehand—and leave Jones to Ben and me."

"Let's hope to hell it works," Musgrave said earnestly. "One way or another, we gotta make that bastard spill his guts."

"It'll work," Starbuck assured him, "if everybody acts like good little soldiers and keeps their mouths shut. But we've got to convince him Ben's word is law! Once he believes that, he'll talk and keep right on talkin'."

"And if he don't?" Rutledge inquired. "What then?"

"Then we're no worse off than we are now."

"What bothers me," Vernon Pryor observed, "is that he might not have all the answers. It's just possible he doesn't know any more than we do."

"In that case," Starbuck said, without irony, "Chub Jones is in for a rough mornin'."

"Suppose we quit jawbonin'," Langham told them, "and find out for ourselves. I figger he's had plenty of time to think about meetin' his maker. You of a mind, Luke?"

"Sooner the better, Ben. Remember what I said, though . . . lots of fire and brimstone."

"Gawddamn, that won't be no trick a'tall!"

Walking away, Langham began thundering orders in a stern, commanding voice. The tree, under which the outlaws waited, suddenly became charged with activity. Several cowhands gathered lariats from the gear strewn about camp, then tossed the ropes over a stout limb and snubbed them firmly around the base of the cottonwood. Other men, meanwhile, saddled five horses and led them forward, halting below the limb. Within a matter of minutes, everything was arranged to Langham's satisfaction, and he nodded toward the outlaws.

"Get 'em mounted!"

Rutledge and Pryor, assisted by a number of the men, jumped to obey. The five outlaws were hoisted aboard the horses, then positioned beneath the dangling ropes. All the while, no one paid the slightest attention to Chub Jones. His eyes glittered like broken glass, and he waited, with a sort of terrified wonderment, for the sixth rope to appear. But he was left, alone and petrified, cowering against the trunk of the cottonwood.

A mounted cowhand rode forward, and one by one

the outlaws had a noose fitted around their necks. Then the four ranchers and Starbuck moved to the rear of the horses, carrying freshly cut switches. Langham held his position, to the front and slightly to one side. He fixed the doomed men with a look of god-like wrath.

"If you boys are prayin' men, you got about ten seconds."

Behind him, formed in a semicircle at the edge of the limb, the cowhands gathered to watch. Their faces were like bronze masks, and they stared at the outlaws in rapt silence. Joe Sixkiller turned in the saddle, pinning Starbuck with a look of cold black hatred, then shifted around and gazed stolidly into the distance. The men on either side of him seemed resigned, their eyes dull and empty. The outlaw nearest the tree wet his pants, tears streaming down his face, and his lips moved in a monotone chant.

"Ooo Jesus, Jesus! Lord God Jesus! Ooo God!"

The last man, somewhat older than the others, laughed. His eyes settled on Langham with a hard stare of contempt. "Mister, you're the sorriest shitheel I ever seen. Hangin' us is lots worse than what we done to you."

"That all you got to say?"

"Yeah, reckon so. 'Cept I shore hope we meet in hell."

"If we do, don't let me catch you stealin' horses."

Langham raised his arm, hesitating a moment, then dropped it. Almost simultaneously, five switches cracked across the horses' rumps, and the animals bolted forward. The outlaws were jerked clear of their saddles, then swung back as the ropes hauled them up short. When the nooses snapped tight, their eyes seemed to burst from the sockets, growing huge and distended, streaked fiery-red with engorged blood vessels. The men thrashed and kicked, dancing frantically on air, as though they were trying to gain a foothold. Slowly, their faces purpled, then grew darker, turned a ghastly shade of blackish amber. Their gyrations spun them in frenzied circles, and one by one their mouths opened, swollen tongues darting and flopping like onyx snakes. A full three minutes passed while they vainly fought the ropes.

Chub Jones, flattened against the tree trunk, stared up as though mesmerized. His face blanched, eyes round as saucers, and he felt his own throat constrict as the outlaws' struggles grew weaker. Even after the men had slowly strangled to death, he couldn't force himself to look away. Their bodies hung limp, necks crooked, swaying gently in the breeze. He clung tighter to the tree, paralyzed with terror, watching.

Langham's voice, harsh and cutting, suddenly broke the stillness. "Awright, boys, one more to go! Get him on his feet!"

Jones cringed away as the four ranchers walked toward him. His eyes fastened on Starbuck, imploring mercy. Then the men pried his hands loose from the tree and roughly jerked him off the ground. A rope whistled over the limb as they carried him forward and held him upright. Someone slipped the noose around his neck, snugged it tight, and the ranchers stepped clear. His wounded knee buckled, but the rope snapped taut and left him teetering on one leg. Behind him, the ranchers relieved a cowhand who was holding the rope, and to his front, Starbuck halted beside Langham. Struck dumb, his face rigid with fear, he saw Langham's arm rise and fall.

The ranchers hauled back on the rope and he was snatched high in the air. Clawing at the noose with his hands, he found himself face to face with one of the hanged outlaws. His eyes bulged, lungs afire, and he gasped for breath, felt his tongue thicken against his teeth. Then, with a sense of deliverance, the rope slackened and he was slowly lowered to the ground. He ripped the noose clear of his throat, sucking great draughts of air, and struggled to hold himself erect on his one good leg. A buzzing in his ears gradually subsided, and he heard his name spoken.

"Are you listenin', Jones?"

Jones took a deep breath, blew it out heavily, took another. His eyes shuttled around, found Langham, and he nodded. His throat was clogged, but he forced himself to answer. "I hear . . . you . . . listenin'."

"By God!" Langham intoned. "You listen good and pay attention! What you just got was only a sample. Next time, you go up and you stay up! Savvy?"

"No." Jones blinked, shook his head. "What're you sayin'—?"

"Why, it's simple, Jones. I'm sayin' you talk or you swing . . . your choice!"

"Talk?" Jones asked hoarsely. "Talk about what?"

"Dutch Henry Horn."

"What about him?"

"Here's the deal," Langham said woodenly. "You tell us where to find Dutch Henry, and you ride out of here a free man. You don't tell us, and we'll stretch your neck like a turkey gobbler. Now you savvy?"

"Dutch never told us nothin'—I swear it! None of us ever knew where he come from or where he went . . . never!"

A harsh bark of laughter. "You're wastin' your breath, Jones. Try again!"

"Honest to God, I'm tellin' you—"

Langham glanced past him and nodded. The rope went taut and Jones was lifted up on tiptoe. He grabbed at the noose, only to be hoisted a few inches higher and left dangling. Langham let him struggle for several seconds, then nodded, and he was once more lowered to the ground.

"Now let's understand each other, Jones. You try to bullshit me again and that's all she wrote! End of the line!"

"I wasn't," Jones gagged. "Don't you see—"

"I see a dead man, unless you start talkin' pretty damn quick."

"You really mean it?" Jones whispered, desperation in his voice. "You'll let me go?"

"You can chisel it in stone," Langham prompted him. "Hell, man, it's Horn we're after, not you! Figger it out for yourself."

Jones threw a quick, guarded glance at Starbuck. "Is he on the level, Luke?"

"Chub, do yourself a favor and spill it. Otherwise, he'll string you up and leave you—"

"Jesus Christ, Luke, you owe me one! I treated you right, and all the time you was foolin' me! So just tell me—straight out—will he let me go?"

"I've known him a long time," Starbuck remarked, "and I've never known him to break his word. I'd advise you to go along, Chub. It's the only chance you've got."

"Awright." Jones bobbed his head. "I'll tell you! But it ain't much, so you gotta gimme your word you'll stick to the deal."

"Goddamn!" Langham scoffed. "You ain't in no position to make demands. Talk up or get strung up, there's your deal!"

Jones swallowed nervously. "Well, first off, you gotta understand Horn's close-mouthed as they come. All I ever learned was what I picked up in bits and pieces."

"Get on with it!"

"Pueblo," Jones said softly. "He's got a hideout somewhere around Pueblo. That's it, all I know."

"Awww for Chrissakes!" Langham muttered. "You and him was thick as fleas! You expect us to believe he never told you anything except Pueblo?"

"He never even told me that! I just put it together from little things he let slip now and then."

"C'mon now, Jones—somewheres around Pueblo?— hell's fire, that'd take in about half of Colorado. You'll have to do better'n that, lots better."

"I wouldn't shit you!" Jones's eyes filled with panic. "I swear to God . . . that's it . . . everything!"

Langham pursed his lips. "What do you think, Luke? Figger he's tellin' the truth?"

"Wouldn't surprise me," Starbuck observed. "Horn's the kind that plays it close to the vest, real skittish."

"Guess that's it, then." Langham studied the fat man a moment, then shrugged. "Hang him."

Jones's protest ended in a gurgled cry as the rope jerked him off the ground. His face contorted in a rictus of agony, and he began the slow dance on thin air. The ranchers snubbed the rope around the tree, then walked back to join Langham and Starbuck. Heavier than the other outlaws, Jones strangled quicker, and within a couple of minutes he hung slack from the limb. When it was over, Langham stood silent for a time, then turned to Gilchrist.

"Oscar, you was always pretty handy at whittlin' " —he paused, nodded at the cottonwood—"I want you to carve me somethin' on that tree."

"Awright," Gilchrist replied. "What do you want carved?"

"Well, since this place ain't got no name, we might as well give it one that's fittin'. So take your knife and do the honors on that tree. We'll call it Hangman's Creek."

Everyone agreed it was a fitting name, and Gilchrist went to work on the tree. The men watched, suddenly sobered by the gravity of all they'd done, and no one spoke for a while. At last, Langham cleared his throat.

"Luke, I reckon it's finished, all except for Horn."

"Funny thing, Ben"—Starbuck knuckled his mustache, thoughtful—"you make that sound like a question."

"Well, the reason I asked," Langham explained, "is because you've done your share and then some. If you'd sooner come on back to the ranch—and take over as foreman again—we'll figger out another way to take care of Horn. Seems to me that's only fair."

"Nooo," Starbuck said slowly. "I guess I'll play out the hand. Always like to finish what I start."

"You're sure now, plumb certain?"

Starbuck nodded, glancing around the campsite. "Hell, it's me that's leavin' you with the dirty chore. Won't be much fun diggin' graves for this bunch."

"We ain't gonna bury 'em!" Langham announced. "We're gonna let the buzzards pick 'em clean and leave the sun to bleach their bones. That'll let their kind know they ain't safe no more . . . not even in No Man's Land!"

Starbuck smiled. "Yeah, I reckon a half-dozen skeletons hangin' from a tree oughta be message enough for anybody."

"If it ain't, we'll damn sure accommodate 'em with a tree of their own."

The men were silent a moment. Then Starbuck regarded the angle of the sun. "Gettin' on toward noon. If I was to leave now, I expect I'd be pretty near the Colorado line before dark."

Langham hawked and spat. "Ain't much to go on. How do you figger your chances?"

"Ask me the next time you see me."

"When'll that be?"

"After I've fixed Dutch Henry's wagon."

"Watch out he don't fix yours first."

"I'll keep my nose to the wind, don't worry."

Starbuck shook hands all around and went to saddle his horse. A while later, leading the gelding, he returned to find Langham supervising as Oscar Gilchrist put the finishing touches on his carving. Everyone else was mounted and preparing to take the trail; on the grasslands to the south, the men were gathering the stolen horses into a single herd. Starbuck paused beside the tree and Langham joined him. There was concern in the older man's eyes, and Starbuck avoided his gaze, nodding instead at Gilchrist's handiwork.

HANGMAN'S CREEK

"Pretty well tells the story, doesn't it?"

"Yeah, reckon it does."

A moment slipped past. "Guess I better head out. Got a fair piece to travel."

"Don't forget your way home, you hear me?"

"I won't, Ben. You can bank on it."

Starbuck stepped into the saddle and rode west along the creek. When he looked back, Langham was still standing there, watching him. On the verge of waving, he suddenly changed his mind. There was something final about a wave—a gesture of farewell rather than a promise of the future—and the old man was concerned enough already on that score. For his part, Starbuck gave little thought to what the future held. His vision was limited to Colorado and Dutch Henry Horn, and beyond that all else was without substance. A thing of conjecture until they'd met one last time.

He tugged his hat down and kneed the gelding into a lope.

CHAPTER NINETEEN

Seated at the desk in his study, Dutch Henry Horn pondered the vicissitudes of life. He was an orderly man, with the discipline of mind and iron will to shape events to suit his own ends. Yet his certainty of purpose was now in disarray, and these days he felt some deep-rooted need to snatch tranquility from the jaws of turmoil.

All morning he'd sat there, abstracted and listless, staring at an opened ledger book. It was the end of the month, time to reconcile his accounts and take stock of the month ahead. But thus far he hadn't touched a pen or made a single entry in the ledger. A stack of bills, along with memos of credit from his bank in Pueblo, lay where he had placed them earlier that morning. Correspondence from the slaughterhouse in Denver and a purchase request from the quartermaster at Fort Lyon also demanded his attention. Still, for all the pressing matters before him, he'd been unable to shake his sluggish mood. His thoughts were elsewhere, on another business venture. The one he'd fled so ingloriously in No Man's Land.

A knock at the door brought him upright in his chair. He took a bill off the top of the stack, dipped his pen in the inkwell, and hunched over the ledger. With a precise stroke, legible as a draftsman's lettering, he began the entry.

"Come in."

The door opened, and Harry Birdwell entered the study. A large, beefy man, with the girth to match his shoulders, Birdwell had served as foreman of Horn's ranch for the past year. Holding a battered Stetson in one hand, he crossed the room and halted in front of the desk.

"Mornin', Mr. Miller."

Horn nodded brusquely. "What is it, Harry?"

"Thought as how I oughta ask you about the payroll."

"What about it?"

"Tomorrow's the first of the month," Birdwell reminded him. "The hands'll be wantin' their pay."

"Goddamn!" Horn glowered. "Why haven't you said something before this?"

"Ain't my place, Mr. Miller. Besides, I never had to say nothin' before."

Birdwell knew next to nothing about the man who called himself Frank Miller. So far as he could determine, Miller had neither family nor past. From his manner of speech, Birdwell pegged him as a Texan; but he volunteered nothing, and his cold attitude hardly encouraged questions. Still, there were many things, bits and pieces gleaned from observation, that told Birdwell all he wanted to know. Frank Miller had a seemingly inexhaustible supply of money; he was a knowledgeable cattleman; and within the last year he had transformed the old Diamond X spread into a topnotch outfit. He was a harsh taskmaster, aloof and demanding, and apparently considered idleness the cardinal sin. Yet he readily delegated responsibility, once a man had earned his trust, and he gave his foreman a free hand with the crew. For Harry Birdwell, that was enough, and he was satisfied to leave certain questions unanswered.

All the same, Birdwell had noted a pronounced change in the Diamond X owner within the last month. He seemed withdrawn, even more distant than usual, and he'd allowed business matters to slide drastically. That was wholly out of character, and it left Birdwell in an uncomfortable position. Today, faced with Miller's churlish attitude, he decided to force the issue. The ranch was suffering, through no fault of his own, and he wasn't about to accept the blame. It was time for a little straight talk.

"Mr. Miller, we got ourselves some problems, and I'm thinkin' it's time we laid 'em out on the table."

"Birdwell—" Horn started, then stopped, took a grip on his temper. "What sort of problems?"

"Just for openers," Birdwell commented, "the beef contracts. We're way past due on both of 'em, and you still haven't give me the go-ahead."

"Why the hell haven't you brought it up before now?"

"I have, and all I got was a deaf ear. Nothin' personal, Mr. Miller, but it's like I told you a minute ago. I'm only the foreman around here."

"The way you're talkin'," Horn said with heavy sarcasm, "maybe you figure you ought to be sittin' behind this desk."

"No, sir, never said nothin' of the kind. All I said was, I'm accustomed to your givin' the orders, and here lately, I ain't been gettin' any."

Horn gave him a dour look. "Watch your step, or you're liable to find yourself ridin' the grub line."

"Anytime you're not satisfied with my work, all you gotta do is say so."

"I'm talkin' about your tone of voice, not your work!"

Horn drew a deep breath, reminded himself to go slow. Only with a supreme effort of will had he made the adjustment from outlaw to rancher. Yet there were times he felt like two men, and it was a constant struggle to beat the callousness of his old self into submission. Men hired to steal horses could be dealt with summarily, even cruelly, but a ranch foreman was another matter altogether. Harry Birdwell was honest and dependable, a proud man, and that made the difference. He had to be treated with respect.

At length, Horn yielded with a casual gesture. "Forget what I said, Harry. I've got a lot on my mind these days, and I guess I'm a little quick to take offense."

"Anything I can help with, Mr. Miller?"

"No, just a personal matter, doesn't concern the ranch."

"Sorta figured as much, after you come back off that last trip, I mean."

Horn regarded him without expression. "What's that supposed to mean?"

"Why, nothin'." Birdwell sensed he'd overstepped himself. "Just that you're generally pretty obligin' after one of them trips. This time you wasn't, that's all."

"Suppose we stick to business and let me worry about my personal affairs. Fair enough, Harry?"

"Hell, suits me. I've got enough trouble of my own."

Birdwell smiled inwardly. The allusion to *personal affairs* convinced him Miller was suffering from a busted romance. All along, he'd thought the trips involved a woman—probably a courtship of long standing—and now the boss had gotten himself jilted. It made perfect sense, and accounted for his virtual seclusion of the past month.

"Now, about these contracts," Horn resumed. "How far are we overdue?"

"Couple of days with the slaughterhouse, and pretty near a week with the army."

"All right," Horn told him, "cut out some beeves and get 'em on the road. Tell your boys to push 'em hard."

"Well, not to pour oil on the fire, but that sorta brings us back to the original problem."

"Which is?"

"The payroll." Birdwell shrugged. "The boys ain't gonna be too happy about hittin' the trail when they ain't been paid."

Horn stared at him for a time, seeming to deliberate. Finally, he tilted back in his chair, fingers steepled. "I'll give you a letter to the bank. You ride into town, pick up the payroll, and then beat it back here. That'll solve that."

Birdwell looked at him, astounded. "You want me to pick up the payroll?"

"Wasn't that what I just said, Harry?"

"Yeah," Birdwell replied doubtfully. "Only I don't get it. You've always looked after that yourself."

"So now I'm sendin' you to look after it for me! Why all the questions?"

"Well . . ." Birdwell shook his head. "I don't know, Mr. Miller. We're talkin' about better'n a thousand dollars."

Horn waved it away. "I trust you, Harry."

"That ain't exactly the point. See, the thing is, Mr. Miller, I'd sooner not take the responsibility. Cows are one thing, but cash money . . . that ain't rightly my bailiwick . . . it's yours."

"Are you tryin' to tell me my business?"

"Nope." Birdwell hesitated, studying the floor. "I'm

only sayin' I don't want no part of the payroll. I wasn't hired on to ride shotgun."

"Jesus Christ! Are you afraid somebody'll rob you?"

"Yeah, I reckon that's partly it."

"Partly?" Horn demanded. "What's the rest of it?"

"Call it anything you want, Mr. Miller. I just ain't partial to handlin' another man's money. That's the way she stacks up, and I'm a little too old to start changin' now."

Horn slammed out of his chair and walked to the window. Before him, spread out along the banks of the Arkansas, some thirty miles southeast of Pueblo, was the Diamond X ranch. His ranch! As large and thriving as any outfit to be found in the whole of Colorado. But it had taken time and vast amounts of money to make it a reality. Now, for the first time in his life, he knew fear. The fear he might lose it all, everything he'd built.

Scarcely two years past, with the Texas Rangers at his heels, Horn had called it quits. At the time, he led a pack of hardcases who specialized in bank and train robberies. Over a period of months, he had enjoyed a long streak of luck, staging successful holdups across the breadth of Texas. But after a near disaster in the town of Waco—and a week-long pursuit by the Rangers—he had decided to end it while he was ahead of the game. With Ranger companies constantly on the prowl, and a telegraph network throughout the state, robbery was fast becoming a hazardous occupation. Severing all ties, he had disbanded the gang and made his way in secret to Colorado.

There, after assuming a new identity, he had determined to go straight. With the money he'd saved, he bought the Diamond X, a ranch that had fallen on hard times during the financial panic of '73. Soon enough, he discovered that ranching, on the scale he envisioned, required resources far beyond his means. The banks, which loaned money only to people who didn't need it, turned him down cold. Faced with the choice of a hardscrabble existence, or devising another source of capital, he had reverted to the way he knew best. But this time, with great forethought and planning, he'd taken care to remain in the background.

The result was a horse-stealing ring, with Chub Jones and some of the old gang members recruited in strictest confidence. None of them knew of the ranch, or his new identity, and his personal risk was limited to the meetings in No Man's Land. The scheme had worked to perfection, and over the past year he'd poured upward of $100,000 into ranch improvements and land acquisition. The Diamond X prospered, his personal fortune seemed assured, and the future had never looked brighter. Perhaps of greater significance, Frank Miller had become a man of prominence and stature throughout southern Colorado. To Dutch Henry Horn, who had ridden the owlhoot all his adult life, it was no small accomplishment. He took immense pleasure in the fact that his Pueblo banker not only loaned him money, but now considered him a personal friend.

Since fleeing No Man's Land, he'd been obsessed by the thought that he might lose all he'd worked so hard to attain. From the volume of gunfire at the campsite, audible for a mile or more as he rode west, he felt reasonably certain the entire gang had been killed or captured. Either way, he had little fear of anyone betraying his whereabouts. None of the men, not even Chub Jones and the other gang leaders, had the faintest notion as to his new life. His fear stemmed instead from the man who had gulled him with such uncanny subterfuge. The one called Starbuck.

Quite obviously, Starbuck was an agent in the employ of one or more cattlemen's associations. It was

common practice these days, and would account for
the large force that had attacked the camp. All the
more apparent, Starbuck was a man of resourceful-
ness and great tenacity. There was little doubt his search
would continue; though the gang itself had been wiped
out, his employers would insist he take the trail of
the ringleader. For that reason, Horn had thought it
best to stay out of sight over the past month. Having
underestimated Starbuck once, he had no intention of
doing so again. By far, the wiser course was to lay low
and allow time to work in his favor.

Yet, in a perverse twist, he'd gradually come to the
conclusion that he owed Starbuck a debt of gratitude.
Except for the debacle in No Man's Land, he might
have gone on with the horse-stealing operation. The
money was simply too tempting to have done otherwise. On the other hand, the Diamond X was pros-
pering, and he no longer had need of outside funds.
So in his greed, he would have continued to run an
unnecessary risk and court disaster on an even larger
scale. All in all, Starbuck had done him a service of
no small consequence. By concentrating solely on
the business of Frank Miller, he would at last put the
old life behind him. And in the process, lay Dutch
Henry Horn to rest.

Thinking about it now, it occured to him that today's
squabble over the payroll was really quite timely.
Harry Birdwell had jolted him out of his funk, and
that was precisely what he'd needed. The fear was
probably all in his mind, anyway, and after a month,
whatever danger might have existed was no longer a
factor. By now, for all his determination, Starbuck
would have concluded that the trail had gone cold.
Even if he persisted, there was no great cause for
alarm. With no leads, nothing to go on, he'd been
working blind from the day of the shootout. The

chances of him wandering into Pueblo were one in a million!

Horn turned from the window. He walked back to the desk and resumed his seat. His manner was now brisk and businesslike, assured.

"Harry, I'll be leaving for Pueblo at first light. You can tell the men they'll have their pay before suppertime."

Birdwell nodded, grinning. "That's fine, Mr. Miller, just fine."

"Get those beeves ready to go, too. While I'm in town, I'll telegraph the slaughterhouse and the quartermaster and hold 'em off with some sort of excuse."

"Good idea," Birdwell agreed. "I'll put the boys to work on a gather first thing in the mornin'."

"One other thing."

"Yessir, what's that?"

"I've been thinkin' it over, and you're right about the payroll. It's a lot of money."

"Folks have been killed for a lot less, Mr. Miller."

"My thought exactly. You never know who you're liable to run across these days."

"Ain't that the goldurn truth!"

"Better safe than sorry, and it occurs to me I've been takin' some damnfool chances carryin' all that money by myself."

Horn considered it a moment, almost as though he were wrestling with some inner decision. Only when he had Birdwell on tenterhooks did he glance up, eyes snapping with authority.

"Harry, I want you to pick out a couple of good men to ride with me tomorrow."

"How d'you mean . . . good men?"

"I mean good with a gun. Damned good!"

CHAPTER TWENTY

The hotel veranda was pleasantly shaded from the noonday sun. Almost hidden in the shadows, Starbuck lazed back, one leg thrown over the arm of a cane-bottomed rocker. His expression was downcast and his mood somber. Smoking one cigarette after another, he sat mired in his own gloom.

Passersby scarcely seemed to notice him. After nearly a month, he'd become something of a fixture on the veranda, and the townspeople had grown bored speculating about his silent vigil. When he'd first ridden into Pueblo, there had been considerable gossip, and a few attempts at tactfully phrased conversation. But the questions were blunted on his reserved manner, and the prying soon stopped altogether. Everyone went back to tending their own business, and now it was as though he'd staked out squatter's rights on the cane-bottomed rocker. Except for an occasional stroll around town, he sat there from early morning until late evening. Seven days a week.

The hotel occupied one corner of Pueblo's main intersection. Anyone entering or leaving town was almost

certain to pass the corner, and the veranda afforded
Starbuck a commanding position. From there, without
making himself conspicuous, he could observe virtually
all the street activity on any given day. At the outset,
having discarded various alternative measures, he had
resigned himself to a long wait. Yet his vigil, pro-
longed beyond anything he might have imagined, had
slowly drained his spirits. He was bored and disheart-
ened and assailed by a growing sense of doubt. He now
thought it quite possible he'd staked out the wrong corner in the wrong town. He seriously questioned that
Dutch Henry Horn had ever set foot in Pueblo.

All morning, his patience worn thin, he'd sat there
considering his options. A month ago, upon entering
Pueblo, none of the ideas had borne up under scrutiny.
Convinced that Horn was using an alias, he knew it
would start the grapevine churning if he went around
town asking questions. All the more so since he had
nothing to go on but the man's description. Once the
talk began, it would have spread quickly, for an in-
quisitive stranger in a small town was prime news. A
tour of the countryside presented even graver problems. Aside from fueling the gossip mill, it was entirely
possible he might stumble across Horn without warning. In light of the man's cunning, that was a situation
to be avoided at all costs. This time out, Starbuck
wanted the odds on his side. Or, if not the odds, then
at least a reasonable chance of walking away alive.
Either way, it was imperative that Horn not be alerted
to his presence.

To compound matters, Starbuck was in a touchy position regarding the law. Whatever face he put on it,
there was simply no argument that would explain away
the slaughter in No Man's Land. With more than
twenty men killed or hung, he couldn't very well enlist
the aid of local peace officers. The law looked askance

on vigilante justice, regardless of the provocation, and horse thieves were no exception. At best, since he was again operating alone, the law would consider him little more than a bounty hunter. At worst, if he attempted to explain the killings in No Man's Land, he would be considered little better than a common outlaw. So that eliminated any chance of support from the town marshal. He was on his own.

Over the past month, Starbuck had pondered that very thought. Seldom reflective, his vigil had left him nothing to do but think, and he'd come to the conclusion he was on his own in many ways. His search for the horse thieves had effectively removed him from the influence of Ben Langham. For the first time in twelve years, he'd answered to no one but himself, felt beholden to no one. Slowly, almost without awareness, his streak of independence had once again exerted itself. Only at the very last, during those final moments in No Man's Land, had he fully realized the extent of the change. Without hesitation, he'd taken command of the ranchers and their men. No counsel was sought, nor had he brooked any interference; he'd simply laid out the plan and told them how to proceed. All the more revealing, none of them, not even Langham, had questioned his judgment. In some curious way, their roles had been reversed, and everyone understood he had assumed leadership of the operation. Looking back, he saw that it had marked a passage in time, a point separating past from present. Perhaps a point of no return.

Still, for all he'd discovered about himself, he found that hindsight had its troublesome moments. He kept thinking back to the words of one of the outlaws they'd hung, the older one who had spoken out near the end. The man had accused them of exacting too harsh a price for simple horse-stealing. At the time, Starbuck hadn't given it much thought. Later, upon reflection, he'd begun to wonder if the man wasn't right. A life in exchange for a horse—even a bunch of horses—was most certainly a stiff bargain. Yet the thief knew the price in advance, and by stealing the horse, he had tacitly accepted the risk. After mulling it over at great length, Starbuck decided it was not so much a matter of right or wrong, but rather whose rights would prevail.

Unless a man defended what was his, there were always other men who would come and take it away from him. The meek of the world, so far as Starbuck could determine, inherited only a portion of the earth. More often than not, it was a hole in the ground, six feet of sod, marked by a headstone attesting to their gentle nature. So a man either defended himself and his property—resorting to violence if necessary—or he forfeited the right to live in peace. Which resulted in dead thieves and honest men who slept fitfully, troubled by bad dreams. Each in his own way paid the price, and since No Man's Land, Starbuck thought perhaps the honest man got the worst end of the deal. His own dreams were of a gallows tree . . . and buzzards . . . and sun-bleached bones. And late at night, awakened in a cold sweat, he wondered if he would ever purge himself of Hangman's Creek. He thought not.

For all his ruminations, however, there wasn't the slightest doubt regarding Dutch Henry Horn. If anyone, it was the ringleader himself who had brought about Hangman's Creek. The terrible price paid there, by the living and the dead alike, demanded justice, swift retribution. Now, more than ever, Starbuck saw himself as the instrument of that retribution. Having arranged the death of so many men, he wanted very much to kill the one who had led them. It seemed somehow important, necessary. A thing not to be left undone.

Yet it was undone!

Staring blankly at the street, Starbuck knew he was at a dead end in Pueblo. The matter was no closer to resolution than it had been a month ago. If he was to find Horn and force a showdown, it wouldn't be accomplished by sitting on his butt in the shade of a hotel veranda. However risky, he must now fall back on the options previously discarded. The first step would be to inquire around town, attempt to turn up a lead that would give him a new direction, a fresh start. Failing that, he would have no choice but to scour the countryside, widening his search to include the whole of Southern Colorado. Up until now he'd played a waiting game, hopeful his quarry would come to him. But it was long past time to switch tactics. Today he must start a hunt, the only kind that would get the job done.

A manhunt.

Starbuck's spirits immediately improved. With a course of action laid out, he felt some of the old vigor return, and decided not to waste so much as another minute. After a quick meal, he would begin making the rounds, asking questions, and it occurred to him the place to start was the town's saloons. Bartenders were a gabby lot, and a steady drinker on a slow afternoon would encourage them to talk.

On the verge of rising, Starbuck caught movement out of the corner of his eye. He glanced to his right and saw three riders pass by the far end of the veranda. A quick onceover, then he looked away, pegging them as cowhands. But suddenly his head snapped around and he looked closer. His jaw fell open as though hinged.

The man in the middle was Dutch Henry Horn!

Struck dumb, Starbuck watched as they rode across the street and halted at a bank catty corner from the hotel. He sat as if nailed to the rocker, unable to move, hands clasping the chair arms so tightly his knuckles turned white. The men dismounted, leaving their horses at the hitch rack, and entered the bank. His mind whirled, and his first thought was that they had him outnumbered. The other men clearly worked for Horn—that much was obvious—for they had trailed him into the bank at a respectful distance. Whether they were cowhands or members of another gang . . .

Starbuck took a tight grip on himself, collected his thoughts. Where they had come from, why they were here—even if they were robbing the bank!—none of that mattered. Only one thing counted. Horn had him outnumbered, and one pistol against three was pure suicide. He needed an edge.

Bolting out of his chair, Starbuck went down the hotel steps and hurried toward the corner. Crossing the street, he walked to a hardware store directly opposite the bank. As he entered, he spotted a rack of long guns on the wall. A clerk approached, and he quickly dug a wad of bills out of his pocket.

"Gimme a shotgun!"

"Yessir." The clerk swept the rack with a proud eye. "We have the finest selection in town. Now, would you prefer—"

"A double-barrel!" Starbuck cut him short. "Any double-barrel, twelve gauge, and some buckshot shells. C'mon, man, move . . . pick a gun!"

The clerk gave him a startled look and pulled a Greener from the rack. Starbuck snatched it out of his hand and tossed the wad of bills on the counter. Watching nervously, the clerk produced a box of shells and stepped back, ignoring the money. Starbuck dumped the shells on the counter, broke open the shotgun, and stuffed a load in both barrels. All the while, glancing through the flyblown window, he'd kept one eye on the bank. As he snapped the Greener closed, Horn emerged, followed by the two cowhands, and crossed the boardwalk.

Starbuck hurried out the door, cocking the hammers on the shotgun. As he stepped into the street, the men circled the hitch rack and separated, moving toward their horses. He halted, planting himself, and threw the Greener to his shoulder.

"Horn!"

The shout brought several passersby to a standstill, and Horn turned. His expression was grave with wonder, a look of raw disbelief in his eyes. For an instant, perfectly motionless, he stared at Starbuck over the barrels of the shotgun. Then his mouth opened in a leather-lunged cry of alarm.

"Holdup! It's a holdup!"

Even as he yelled, Horn spun and dove headlong beneath one of the horses. On either side of him, the cowhands reacted instantly, clawing at their guns. Starbuck hesitated, saw the pistols coming level, and ripped out a command.

"No! Wait!"

A slug whistled past his ear, and another tugged at his shirtsleeve. The cowhands had fired almost simultaneously with his yell, and now they frantically thumbed the hammers on their pistols. Starbuck triggered both barrels within the space of a heartbeat. The scattergun erupted with a blinding roar and sent a double-load of buckshot hurtling across the street. The cowhands were flung backward, almost as though their backbones had been snatched clean, and slammed to the ground. Peering through a dense cloud of gunsmoke, Starbuck broke open the Greener, then remembered he hadn't brought along extra shells. He tossed the shotgun aside and jerked his Colt.

Advancing on the fallen men, he spotted movement beyond the horses, which were now rearing and fighting to break free of the hitch rack. A quick stride took him past the corner, and he saw Horn sprinting west along the sidestreet. He snapped a hurried shot and splinters flew off the building above Horn's head. Ducking low, Horn raced to the end of the building and turned south into an alley.

Starbuck ran after him, vaguely aware of faces in the bank window and men crouched in doorways. At the alley, he paused and took a cautious peek around the corner of the building. A bullet pocked the earth at his feet, followed by the report of a gunshot. An instant later, Horn darted from behind a pile of rubbish at the far end of the alley. Starbuck threw up the Colt, firing as he caught a blur in the sights, and missed. Before he could fire again, Horn had crossed the street and vanished into a small adobe.

Walking swiftly, Starbuck moved through the alley. He kept his eyes on the adobe, shucking empties and reloading as he went. When he reached the end of the alley, he was at the edge of the business district. He flattened himself against the last building and slowly inspected the adobe. It was a Mexican cantina, set off by itself on the outskirts of town. The door stood ajar, and inside he saw movement, heard the chatter of excited voices. A sudden hunch told him Horn was no longer in the cantina.

Crossing the street, he hurried to the rear of the adobe, and eased around the corner. There was a back door, which was closed, and several yards away stood a one-holer outhouse. Beyond that was a stretch of open ground, then a cluster of adobe houses. He saw no one, and for a moment he debated whether to try

the back door. Then his gaze was drawn to the outhouse, and his eyes narrowed. The door was shut and
the latch bar firmly in place. But the latchstring
stopped swaying even as he watched. Someone was in
the outhouse.

With a casual glance around, Starbuck started toward the opposite side of the adobe. In mid-stride, he
suddenly whirled, leveling the Colt, and drilled a hole
through the outhouse door. Thumbing the hammer
back, he drew a steady bead on the door, then called
out in a hard voice.

"Dutch Henry, you got a choice! Come out with
your hands up, or I'll turn that privy into a sieve."

"Hold off, Starbuck! I'm comin' out, you win!"

The latch bar lifted and the door creaked open.
Horn stood in a spill of sunlight, his arms raised above
the door sill. He blinked, watching Starbuck with a
sardonic expression.

"You're a regular bulldog once you get started,
aren't you?"

"Toss your gun out of there, Dutch! Slow and easy,
nothin' fancy."

"I laid it on the seat before I opened the door."

"Then lower your hands—one at a time!—and
you'd better come up empty."

"Hell, I know when I'm licked." Horn lowered his
left hand, palm upraised. "See, no tricks and no—"

His right arm dropped in a flash of metal. Starbuck
triggered three quick shots. The slugs stitched a neat
row straight up Horn's shirtfront, bright red dots from
belly to brisket. Knocked off his feet by the impact,
Horn crashed into the back wall of the privy, then sat
down on the one-holer. A pistol fell from his hand, and
his head tilted at an angle across one shoulder. His
eyes were opaque and lusterless, staring at nothing.

Starbuck walked forward and halted at the door. He

lowered the hammer on his Colt, gazing down on the dead man. He thought it ironic that Horn would have attempted the very trick he'd once pulled on Sam Tate. A smile tugged at the corner of his mouth, and he slowly shook his head.

"You should've known better, Dutch. You sure should've."

"Hands up!"

Starbuck tensed, but the voice behind him was cold with menace. "Go ahead, sonny, just gimme an excuse."

With great care, Starbuck dropped the Colt and raised his arms. He glanced over his shoulder and caught the gleam of a tin star. Though he'd never spoken with the town marshal, they had occasionally exchanged nods during the past month. Now, as the lawman moved forward, he slowly turned.

"What's the problem, Marshal?"

"You're under arrest."

"On what charge?"

"The murder of Frank Miller."

"The murder"—Starbuck stopped, suddenly frowned —"who the hell's Frank Miller?"

"He's right behind you, sonny . . . sittin' on the crapper."

CHAPTER TWENTY-ONE

"Yessir, sonny, you're a mighty lucky fellow."

"I sure wish you'd quit callin' me 'sonny.'"

"I will, soon as you get the hell outta my town!"

Walt Johnson unlocked the door and swung it open. Starbuck glanced around the cell, his home for the last three weeks, and stepped into the corridor. With a dour grunt, the lawman turned and walked toward the front of the jail. His gray hair and stout build belied his reputation with a gun. A man of few words, he was hard-eyed and astringent, and possessed little or no tolerance for lawbreakers. He had an even greater dislike for honest citizens who took the law into their own hands. High on his list at the moment was Luke Starbuck.

In his office, Johnson moved to his desk and opened a bottom drawer. He removed Starbuck's gunbelt and laid it on top the desk. He stood for a moment, studying the holstered Colt, then glanced up at Starbuck.

"You load that thing before you hit the town limits and I'll toss your ass back in jail."

Starbuck smiled. "Thought you'd be glad to get rid of me, Marshal."

"You just mind what I'm tellin' you. I don't want nobody else killed, and you'd do yourself a big favor by seein' it my way."

"Seems to me it's the other way round."

"Yeah, how so?"

"What if someone braces me before I make it out of town?"

"They won't," Johnson assured him. "Not that I'd blame 'em, but I'll see to it you aren't bothered."

"Still stuck in your craw, isn't it?"

"Folks around here thought a lot of Frank Miller."

"How about Dutch Henry Horn?" Starbuck replied. "Or don't that part count?"

"Guess it all depends on whose ox was gored. He kept his nose clean in Pueblo, and that's the way folks remember him."

"What about yourself, Marshal? You keep sayin' folks, but I've got an idea you're still wearin' blinders, too."

"I'm a lawman," Johnson noted sternly. "Sometimes I don't like the way things work out, but I enforce it all the same."

Starbuck was forced to concede the point. His first night in jail, a lynch mob had formed on the street, demanding Frank Miller's killer. Only Walt Johnson, armed with a sawed-off shotgun, had dissuaded them. With chill dignity, he'd warned the crowd they would have to kill him to get the prisoner. The citizens of Pueblo knew him to be a man of his word, and there was no more talk of lynching.

Yet there was every likelihood the prisoner would be brought to trial and hung legally. Johnson had never heard of Dutch Henry Horn, nor was he impressed by Starbuck's tale of a horse-stealing ring. It all sounded improbable and highly farfetched, particularly as it involved Frank Miller, one of the area's leading ranchers and a man of impeccable reputation. Still, in his own hard way, the marshal believed that justice afforded the accused certain rights. Fending off the county prosecutor, he set about checking Starbuck's story.

A telegraph inquiry to the sheriff in Fort Worth brought an astounding reply. There was, indeed, a horse-stealing ring. Some weeks past, the Panhandle Cattlemen's Association had delivered more than fifty head of stolen stock to the sheriff's office. How they had come by the horses remained a mystery—for the ranchers were stubbornly silent on that score—but there was no doubt the brands had been altered. Moreover, the ranchers vouched for one Lucas Starbuck, and confirmed that he was employed by the Association as a range detective. Almost as an afterthought, the sheriff's reply verified an outstanding warrant on a man known as Dutch Henry Horn. A wanted poster, bearing the man's likeness, would be forwarded by mail.

The wire itself caused a furor. It substantiated Starbuck's story and indicated he might very well be telling the truth about Frank Miller. The townspeople, however, refused to believe the allegations. There was a concerted effort to bring him to trial, and only at the marshal's insistence was a postponement granted to await the wanted circular. When it arrived, some two weeks later, Pueblo was rocked to the foundation. The likeness it bore was excellent, and erased all doubt.

Frank Miller and Dutch Henry Horn were one and the same. One man leading two lives.

Starbuck was cleared regarding Horn, but it took another week to resolve the matter of the dead cowhands. A certain element in town was of the opinion that a bounty hunter—even though he'd escaped the noose for the murder of Frank Miller—most assuredly deserved to be hung for shotgunning innocent men. In time, and again at Walt Johnson's insistence, witnesses to the shootout came forward. It was established that the cowhands had fired first, under the mistaken impression Starbuck was a robber, and that he'd acted in his own defense. The killings were ruled justifiable homicide.

Acting at the marshal's request, the court had also ruled that Starbuck spend one last night in jail. Walt Johnson, sensing the mood of the town, thought it best to release his prisoner at sunrise, while most of Pueblo still slept. In that, Starbuck heartily agreed, and now, as they faced one another across the desk, it occurred to him that he was in the marshal's debt. He was having trouble with the words.

"I'm not much on thanks"—Starbuck faltered, doggedly went on—"but I want you to know I'm obliged. You've treated me square."

Johnson frowned. "You don't owe me nothin'. I was just doing what I'm paid to do." He paused, considering. "Tell you what, though . . . you do me a favor and we'll call it even."

"Name it."

"Don't you never come back to my town."

Starbuck laughed. "You can take it to the bank, Marshal. As of today, Pueblo's scratched off my list."

Walt Johnson nodded, and led the way outside. Starbuck's horse was tied to the hitch rack, with his bedroll and a bag of provisions strapped in place. There was an uncomfortable moment, then Starbuck smiled and patted the holstered Colt.

"You said the town limits, didn't you?"

"Sonny, let me give you a last piece of advice. Put

some distance between yourself and town before you stop to load that thing. You'd be surprised how quick folks forget once you're gone."

"Yeah, I reckon you're right."

The men looked at each other, then nodded. There was no offer of a handshake, nor was it expected. Starbuck mounted, and as dawn gave way to sunrise, he rode past the hotel. At the edge of town, he twisted around in the saddle and saw the solitary figure still watching him. With a mock bow, he swept his hat off, but there was no response from the lawman. He laughed aloud, then swatted his horse across the rump and turned away from Pueblo.

A few miles out of town, he reined to a halt on the north bank of the Arkansas. On the opposite side of the river, the road snaked south toward the Staked Plains. By continuing on, he would eventually strike the headwaters of the Canadian. From there, it was a matter of a hard day's ride to the Panhandle and the LX range. Fall roundup would be underway, and if he chose to do so, he could resume his duties as foreman within the week. Ben Langham had made that clear when they parted in No Man's Land. Yet the alternative was still open. An experienced range detective was always in demand, and with Hangman's Creek to his credit, he could find work wherever he chose to ride.

Anywhere, in any direction.

Thoughtful, he pulled the Colt, thumbed the hammer to half-cock, and opened the loading gate. As he stuffed shells into the chambers, it occurred to him that the decision was not all that difficult. Even in random moments, he seldom gave any consideration to the old life. His thoughts of the LX and Ben Langham were more like memories, and try as he might, he could no longer summon an image of Janet

Pryor in his mind's eye. Events and time had dulled that life, altered all the days ahead. To whatever purpose, he'd been brought to the point of no return.

A slow grin creased his mouth. Another image flashed through his mind, vivid and clear, shiny-bright. He saw Lisa, radiant with bawdy laughter, rushing to greet him. Her arms were outstretched, and she hurried across the floor of the Comique, calling his name. The image evoked warm stirrings, a sense of need, and he knew everything else could wait. There was time enough ahead, a lifetime.

Starbuck lowered the hammer on an empty chamber and holstered the Colt. Gathering the reins, he feathered the gelding's ribs and turned downstream. He rode into the sunrise toward Dodge.

Whistling softly to himself.